A CROSS TO BEAR Book 4

KATHI S. BARTON

This is a work of fiction. Names, characters, places, and incidents are products of the author's imagination or are used fictitiously and are not to be construed as real. Any resemblance to actual events, locations, organizations, or persons, living or dead, is entirely coincidental.

World Castle Publishing, LLC
Pensacola, Florida
Copyright © 2023 Kathi S. Barton
Paperback ISBN: 9798891260689
eBook ISBN: 9798891260696
First Edition World Castle Publishing, LLC, October 9, 2023
http://www.worldcastlepublishing.com
Licensing Notes
Cover: Karen Fuller
Editor: Karen Fuller

Chapter 1

Amelia had a whole new respect for her mother. She'd been the grand witch of all witches when she'd been alive. Now that Mom was gone, she'd given her all to her. Having a monthly meeting with some of the coven would make a grown woman sob. But she was determined to make this work even if she had to kill the lot of them.

When someone nudged at her from a link, she paused in her nearly destroying the witch in front of her. Pausing, she thought, was a good thing too. Otherwise, she might well have enjoyed herself too much and taken out the entire room. Amelia knew that people would be mad about it, but she was just pissed off enough today to do it.

"You're in a mood today." She smiled when it was Jamie, mate to Mark, the oldest brother and king of the bears to the Cross bruin, who spoke to her.

"*My goodness, what is she going on about? Something about housing? I wouldn't think you guys would have that much trouble with housing. Just poof, you have a house.*"

"Yeah, but that's a big no-no with being a witch. We can't use our magic to make our lives easier. Not that everyone doesn't do this already to a small degree, but there is a limit even on what I will approve. This one, in particular, is wholly aware of what the rule is but has been working on loopholes — that I must admit are pretty clever — to get her neighbor to turn over her house to her. It's bigger, she says and just what she needs to hold her monthly meetings. But it's the appliances, as well as the large master bedroom, that she wants more. Also, there is a large pool out back that she thinks her family will enjoy more than hers would. It's not going to happen." They both laughed at her, already knowing what she was going to say to the woman. *What can I do for you, my dear friend?*"

"*You know what I did for the government, right?*" She asked her if she was still working for them, finding people that needed to be found and dealt with. "*When they beg and pay me a shit ton of money, I'll work for them. In this one, Jamie is going to help me out as well. She has this freaky ability that allows her to change into the littlest things and get in and out without anyone* being the wiser. Anyway, I digress. I need your help with the earth. I could have asked Frazier because he can do it too, but he's having entirely too much fun, and you're not. So I thought that I'd distract you with a project."

"No, I'm not having fun. However, I do feel as if I'm missing something here. Like I'm being tested or something." Jamie asked her to hold on, she'd look. After a few minutes of her asking questions to, Mable, the woman in front of her, Jamie, spoke to her again. "You're kidding? I know you're not, but I can see my mother doing this. Every day, I find things that I'd like to take her to task about. I wouldn't, but there are days. So they want to piss me off with bogus requests so that I will get so fed up and tell them I didn't care what they did. Slick work around if you can get them to make me pissy. Which I am, but now I'm going to be here all fucking day and hand out charges against them until this is finished. In the meantime, I can help you too. Whatever you need from me."

"Great. There is a visitor in town who is making issues. Usually, I wouldn't care, but when I had to go into town earlier this morning, he nearly knocked me down when he stomped by me. I got like a reading from him. He's looking for his sister and her kid. I haven't any idea why he's pissy about that. His mind was too focused on finding *them rather than why."* She asked Jamie if she had a visual of him. *"I do. Frazier said you work better when you have something like that. When he turned around to cuss me out, I got a good look at his face and the gun he was packing. He's not anymore, by the way. I had Sunny take it from him. She couldn't get a read on him either. He is seriously pissed off right now. I just wanted to rape his mind, but I think it's important to figure out what he's doing rather than killing him off with my magic."*

"Okay. You think of him, and I'll have a look. From there, I can trace him backward to — how far do you need me to go?" Jamie told her that at least until she found out what his anger was about. *"If I see the face of his sister or her kid, I'll go that route as well. If they're not guilty of anything and he's just a prick, I don't want to allow them to be hurt. Can you...I don't know, keep listening to this woman and hint at what I should be saying when she pauses?"*

"Does she ever pause?" They both laughed, and she said that she'd do it. *"Thanks for this. I hope you can at least find out something. You've helped me a great deal, and I want to return the favor."*

It only took her a few seconds to find the man. He was sitting in a restaurant having a cup of coffee. Amelia hated coffee with a passion. While she was drinking hot tea with Frazier nightly, she didn't care all that much for the store-bought brand at all. It was his granny's tea that she had fallen in love with. But since she and her mate, Frasier's grandda, had died, Amelia had not asked for any of it, thinking that they'd want to keep it around, but she could go for some of her fall special right now.

Getting into his mind, she found that he was an angry sort of shit, pissed off about nearly everything that didn't go his way—which was usual because he was an idiot of the first degree. While searching for the cause of his over-the-top anger, she looked around for his reason for wanting to find his sister. It could be nothing more than she was a bitch and had said something to him this morning, but she—just as she was making up stories that might have pissed the man off, she found the source of his anger. It wasn't good. Nor were some of the other things that she'd been able to find out in the man's mind.

"Jamie?" She said she was there. *"There is a body in a gully near the entrance to the Pigeon Forge area. Not far from the mile marker that leads people back to Gatlinburg. He's been there for a while, at least a couple of months. Decomposed and been shot three times. There won't be an identification on him, but his name is Nathan*

Webb. He's somehow connected to Dave Farley's sister. By the way, he's the angry shit. I can't find where he killed his brother-in-law, but he does know where his body is. And if you have someone look at his body hard enough, you'll find enough evidence on him to make a case that Shithead had done it, I believe."

"That has him angry? Oh well, that's the man that I was supposed to find any way that the Feds asked me to look for. Webb has been missing from his home for about that long, too. Since he's an attorney representing some high-profile federal cases, the Feds want him found now rather than later. They're not going to be happy with the news, I'm afraid." Amelia said she was still looking. *"You might want to tune into your meeting before you do that. Mabel is thinking that you're agreeing with her proposal for her to take the house because you've not said anything in a while. She's a cow, and you should lay down the law and tell her how it's not going to happen. Even with magic, people are greedy fucks, aren't they."* Amelia looked at Mabel while agreeing with Jamie.

"I think that you've gone on about this quite enough, Mabel. You knew when you got here that I wasn't going to agree with you. You've been a waste of my time and that of the others here, and I don't appreciate it. You will live in the house that belongs to you and leave your neighbor alone. If I hear that you are tormenting her again, I will have you pay a hefty fine for pestering her about anything at all. And I don't mean materially, either. I will strip you of some of, if not all, of your magic." She looked around the room. "If you think that I'm going to do what my mother has done in the past, then you are sadly mistaken about that. I will hear each and every case, and I will, good or bad, pass judgement on you. If you are here to waste my time, to piss me off so that I walk away? You don't know me very well. I will be here until every appearance is heard. Do I make myself clear?"

Six of the witches gathered up their things and left. Two more were nodding like they were happy this was the way she was going to handle things from now on but left as well. As the eight remaining witches sat there, Amelia told them that she wasn't going to be listening to anyone wanting to increase their wealth by means of magic that was against their bylaws. In the end, everyone in the room left, and she was finally able to concentrate on the man.

"Thanks for leading me right to Webb. Now, if you could find out where Farley's sister is and if she and her child are all right, I'd feel a good deal better. I have no

idea why, but I have a feeling that this isn't going to bode well for her in the end. Not if he's that angry still after a couple of months." Amelia told her that she'd found the source of his anger. *"I'm not going to like it, am I?"*

"Probably not. Nathan, the man in the gully, was an attorney for Madeline Farley, Dave's sister, in getting her child support for the kid. I hate it when people do that. If you can't afford a kid or don't want one, then don't create them. There are methods of keeping that from happening. She goes by – hang on. She has three children, Jamie. They're triplets. Two daughters and a son. Anyway, Maddy needs her child support. Baby Daddy is behind by about eight years now. Burney Archer, their father, just stopped working above board so that he'd not have to pay her for the kid's needs. Nathan and Maddy had been friends since before they started kindergarten together. He was helping her pro bono. Sadly, it cost him his life." She asked if she knew why her brother killed him. *"Dave has never liked Webb. He was a brilliant attorney and a good friend of Maddy. Plus, he'd been helping her hide from the man. Why hiding? I don't see it in his mind, but I'm assuming that it has something to do with the fact that he knows Archer from prison, and they're working together on this. They were prison inmates together and, like minds, and all became good friends."*

"So this shit killed the attorney that is helping his sister get food on the table for his two nieces and nephew because he didn't like him? You do know that is one of the stupidest reasons I've ever heard for a reason to kill someone, don't you? Not to mention treating his own flesh and blood this way. Christ, I hate people." Amelia laughed and said for as long as she's been around, that one is way up on the top of her list, too. "Do you happen to know where Maddy and the kids are? I mean, is he even in the right area to find them?"

"Let me have a search around. She's a pretty little thing, by the way." Amelia found the woman easily enough, but finding the kids was a little more difficult. Each time the woman bounced from hiding place to hiding place, she didn't have the children with her. Being ten, she figured that they'd have a good handle on being able to care for themselves, but she really didn't know that many children. "She's good at hiding them away, that's for sure. And she is in town. She works three jobs right now, each of them a restaurant — to which there are an incredible amount of them around here that is forever hiring. Dishwasher for two of them, and she cleans rooms for a bed and breakfast just up the road from where her brother is enjoying coffee. Right now, she's at one of the restaurants washing dishes. She'll be getting off soon.

And it's payday for her. Poor woman. She isn't making much. When this is over, I'm going to find her and help her out."

"I have him now. One of the officers who is helping me today is going to be watching him for the next few hours. By tonight he won't be able to take a shit without the Feds knowing the weight, size and what it consisted of. He's staying at one of the larger hotels just off the main drag in Gatlinburg." Amelia said she'd not known that she had that much pull. *"Neither did I, to be honest, but once I told them that he killed Webb, a high-profile attorney, they stepped right in and took over. Fine by me. I would have just killed Dave right off the bat, and that would be the end of it."*

Still looking for the kids, she found four other hiding places that they'd been using over the last month. Each time they moved, it was as if they knew that Dave was close on their tail. They'd leave quickly and quietly. Sometimes, the kids would simply bug out of a hiding place before their uncle showed up an hour later. Never any less than that, either. Just as she was moving to the next place, she hit paydirt.

"Found them. Christ, Jamie. They're behind the Gatlinburg Crockett's Breakfast Camp in one of the empty buildings. It has electricity and heat but nothing else. It's

on Parkway. They're going to be caught if — never mind, they're on the move again. They heard some kid taking the trash out or something and have hidden again. They're all right, but I'd really like it if you were to pop there and get them. Take Mark with you. I don't want any of you hurt because they're digging in the dumpsters." She watched as the kids seemed to know just what they were looking for. "They're smart as tacks, those three. Or their mother taught them well. Either way, they're not just eating people's leftovers from their plates, thankfully. They've found some pancake mixes that are expired. Also, they've found a bag of apples, some other spices and some kind of canned meat. I think it's ham. Now they have some syrup that they're putting in their backpacks. They're resourceful. I'll give them that."

"Do you know where they are headed?" She told her that they'd been staying in one of the many empty shops long that lane and would more than likely hit another empty building before nightfall. "Okay. I'm going to go up Parkway and pop into the first empty building I come to, hopefully ahead of them. This might turn out badly if they scream or something. What are you going to do?"

"Get their mom. I'll get her and then bring her with me to meet up with you guys. I just realized that one of the *girls is hurt. I don't know how or anything. I'm focusing more on keeping up with Maddy for now."* Jamie said that sounded like a good idea. *"I'll see you soon. But please be careful. I don't want anything to happen to you either."*

Amelia used her considerable magic to close up the building that she was in as she made her way to the restaurant where Maddy was working. Just as she was ready to come out of the bathroom where she had popped, there was a shot fired in her direction.

It took her a few minutes to find out where the shots had come from. Then too much time for her to find Maddy. Just as she feared, it was she who had been shot. And it was bad, too.

She couldn't leave with Maddy, not with her wounds the way that they were. Her life blood was pouring out of her even as Amelia was trying to save her. Maddy had been shot by someone coming from the dining area, looking for her, no doubt. There were people screaming and running around like they'd never seen blood before. Having enough, she entered the room and looked around to see what she had to work with.

It looked like she was going to bleed out if someone didn't get their heads out of their asses, so

Amelia entered the brouhaha and started barking orders. No one seemed to understand that she didn't work there but did what she told them. Telling Jamie what was going on, she gave her just enough magic to keep her alive. That was the best she could do with all the witnesses running around.

"Maddy has been shot twice. It's going to be touch and go here for a little bit. She was shot once in the head and then in the chest. Get the kids, and I'll meet you at the hospital. I can't tell who shot her as I've never been close enough to the fucking bastard that's her brother to tell. But I have his scent now. He's mine." Jamie asked if she thought she'd be a while. *"Not on my end. But there is…Oh damn, Jamie. I found your officer. He's dead. And it looks like Dave boy shot and killed him. I can see his trail now, and it was him. Dave shot his sister, too. I'm so sorry. I can't save him. He was already gone when I found him. But I'm working on Maddy."*

"Are you coming in the ambulance with her?" She said that she could. *"I'll make sure that you can. Just be careful. Dave is on the run again, I'm assuming. We'll find him. And when we do, he's going to pay. I'm with the kids. I will have to tell them something so that — "*

"Hang on. Maddy is talking to me." Leaning down to hear what she had to say, Amelia told her that

they were picking up the kids right now. Nodding, she told her the word that she'd have to know in order for them to believe her. Once she had given it up, Maddy closed her eyes. Amelia gave the young woman a bit more magic to help her and spoke to Jamie. *"Tell them that their mother is hurt and going to live, but the code word for them to trust you is…you're not going to believe this, Jamie, but it's 'Minnie.' Just that. Minnie."*

~*~

Thad didn't have any idea why he trusted the people who had…well, his mind wouldn't allow him to think too hard about how they'd gotten to the hospital. The big man, his name was Mr. Gibb, had wrapped his arms around his waist, and they were suddenly at the hospital. He might well have hurt the man, even if he'd only been able to kick him, but his sisters were there too and didn't seem to be in any kind of fear. That was good enough for him. For now, anyway.

The two people holding onto them were Miss Sunny and Miss Jamie. He looked over at the man who had entered the emergency department by the sliding door. Like a normal person would, he wanted to point out but didn't. He sat down beside them as they were waiting in the waiting room and looked him right in the eyes. Mom had told them that it was a good person that could do that.

"My name is Mark Cross. This is my wife, Jamie, who has helped you. This is my sister-in-law Sunny and my brother, but not her husband Gibb. You've introduced yourself to them?" All three of them told him that they had. "Good. All right. My sister-in-law, Amelia, is with your mom. They're on their way in by ambulance right now. Did you know that your mom had been hurt?"

"Yes, sir." Thad looked at his sisters when they nodded at him. He didn't know if this was a good idea or not, but they had all agreed by talking about it through their own special link. "We've been on the run for a bit now. Mom is about a step ahead of her brother all the time, but I guess today he was too good. We've been moving around a lot, so no one could find us. Dave, that's his name. He's not a very nice person. Is mom going to be all right?"

"Yes. She's in good hands. In the event that you didn't notice, we're all magical. Amelia is a witch and is staying next to your mom while she's on her way in. Using her magic, she's made sure that your mom will be all right. She won't allow anything to happen to her while she's being taken care of. All right?" Thad nodded and looked at his sisters Belle and Maria again. "I've been told that one of you is hurt. This is a good time to be fixed up while we're here. No one will get to the four—and that would include your mom—of you while we're with you. And we're not leaving you at all."

"Belle has been hurt. She hurt her ankle two nights ago when we were on the run. I tried to wrap it up for her, but it's still hurting her." Belle showed Mark her ankle when he asked. All he did was touch it, and Belle didn't seem to be in pain anymore. "Thank you for that. She's been hurting so much that I was worried about her. Does that work for all kinds of stuff, Mr. Mark?"

"Yes. Are you hurt?" He wanted to tell him that he was hungry, and that hurt, too, but he knew that wasn't what he meant. So all he did was lift his pant leg up to show him the bled-through paper towel that was on the wound he had on his leg. Thad had been keeping clean with paper towels since the night it had happened. The infection was nasty smelling, and he'd get all sweaty at night when it hurt the worse. "That's a nasty cut, Thad. How did you get that? If you don't mind me asking."

"We were almost caught a couple of weeks

ago. Mom was going to get me something to put on it today when she got paid, but I guess her brother caught up with her. I got hurt because I was going back to get the food that we'd left when we ran just when Dave showed up. He was really mad that he'd missed us again. I got the cut from coming out of a screened-in window and didn't get the food that we had there. We had to start over again with supplies."

Thad decided right then that he was never going to call Dave his uncle again. The man had been tormenting them since he and his sisters were little. All on account of the little bit of something that the three of them had, and he wanted them to work for him. It was Maria who started talking to Mark then.

"We can see things. Not really anything that is important to us. Contests, mom calls them, like ball games and horse races. We see who the winner is. We can also see the score or times the horses come in to win on the contest too. You know, when it's over." Mark didn't say anything as he pulled the paper towel completely off his wound. "But Belle, she can see when we're going to be caught, and we move then. It's only a little bit of time, but bugging out all the time is hard to do. Especially when we don't have food again. I'm powerful hungry, Mr. Mark."

"I just bet you are. And I'll get you all something to eat after we talk to the doctor here. I don't know what they'll find when they examine you, but you'll be safe as you would be with your own mother. I promise." Jamie looked at his leg then. "That really is a nasty cut. However, I'd feel better if you were to get it cleaned up before we fix you up. All right? I mean, there might be something in the wound that will only keep festering if I were to heal you like Mark did your sister. No one will know that you're here, nor that you're hurt. I won't even tell your mom until she's better. If that's okay?"

"Yes. I don't want her to worry. She hates leaving us to get some work, but we need stuff, too. Food most important, I guess. We've gotten good at knowing who throws out the best things that we can eat." Having someone helping them, even if they were strangers, nearly made him cry, he was so relieved. He and his sisters had been trying so hard not to show their mom how afraid they were, and he thought that was stressing them out more. "Mom had to take us back from him about a year ago. It was our birthday, and he'd been in the house. I don't think he'd been invited or anything. He just came into the house and beat the snot out of our mom. After he drugged us, he took us to the racetrack and made us tell him the winners and stuff. It's cheating, and we know it, so we didn't want to help. But we'd had no choice as he told us that if we didn't help, he'd find our mom and kill her to make us do it. Mom got us from him with the help of her friend, Nathan. My biological father, he's a deadbeat, Mom said, and he owes Mom a lot of money that could be going for us having insurance and a car to get around in. I don't know why we'd need either of those, but Mom sure does think it would make a difference for us."

Thad realized how angry he sounded and apologized to Mr. Mark. He told him he'd be angry too if someone that is supposed to be caring for him and didn't do their job. Then he told him that they'd be staying with him and his wife until they could get to the bottom of things. He looked at his sisters to see if they were all right with that and noticed that Belle was staring at Mr. Gibb.

"What's wrong?" Thad didn't know what he could do to the man if he was going to hurt them, but they knew how to run, and they would too if it came to his sisters being safe. He might well be only ten years old, but he was street mean, as his momma called it. "Belle? What's wrong? Has Mr. Gibb or any of the others hurt you in any way?"

"No. Not at all." She finally looked at him. "We should stay with Mr. Gibb. He needs to get to know us all better."

Thad didn't know what was going on, but if Belle told him that he needed to boil his toes in oil, he'd do it. She'd never been wrong about stuff before. Maria could, too, tell them when they'd be safe someplace, but not nearly as often as Belle did.

"Gibb?" He only looked over at his brother and shrugged. It was then that Mr. Mark burst out laughing. "I think I get it. All right. As soon as Amelia and your momma get here, we'll test out this theory. All right?"

Mr. Gibb only smiled and looked at the three of them. Again, he didn't know what was going on, but he figured that sooner or later, he'd talk to Belle and find out what was going on. When the big doors opened to the sound of sirens, he stood up with his sisters. His leg was hurting so bad by then that he nearly fell. And would have had Mr. Gibb not grabbed him up and held him in his arms.

It was their mom. He wanted to go to her so badly, and he might well have if Mr. Gibb hadn't told him that he'd be getting in their way of taking care of her. He only agreed with not going to her when Belle told him that she was going to be just fine.

"They're going to take her right up to surgery, and then they'll admit her." The woman who had been getting out of the ambulance came to kneel in front of them. "You must be Thad. And your sisters are Belle and Maria. Your mom was so worried about you that she made me promise that I'd keep an eye on you all for her. I know that this is a great deal to put on you right now, but you couldn't be in better hands than you are with my family. We'll take the best care of you, and when your momma is better, we'll take care of her, too."

"I trust them too." A nurse came to get him and Mr. Gibb. Amelia asked what was going on. Thad showed her his leg. "I have a cut on my leg that they're going to look at. I don't want my mom to know until she's better. All right?"

"Good idea." She looked up and over his shoulder at Mr. Gibb. "I think that all of you should be checked out while you're here. What do you think, Gibb? That way, when your mom is better, and she will be, we can tell her that you're all in the best of health."

"Excellent. What do you say, girls? Ready to

make sure that you're all healthy with your brother?" His sisters followed him back to the emergency room without a bit of complaining. It made him feel better just knowing that they were in good hands.

Once they were back there, it was as if there wasn't anyone else in the world around but the three of them to be seen. He was taken to x-ray after being put in a gown. Mr. Gibb stayed with him while his sisters were with Miss Jamie.

"While you're gone, Thad, I'll see about getting a bigger room so that the three of you can be together while here." He thanked him. "I got you now, buddy. I promise you. You and your sisters are going to be just fine. I swear to you."

Thad couldn't help it. He started to cry. It was so wonderful to have someone taking over all the things he'd been doing since he and his family had been on the run. Mr. Gibb didn't say anything while he held him but told Belle and Maria that stress and pain will make even grown men upset. After a few minutes of just holding onto someone stronger and willing to help them, he was taken to the other department to see about his leg.

When he got back to his room, there were two more beds in the room with his sisters on them.

Belle was asleep, and Maria was looking at what he thought was Mr. Gibb's phone. He was in so much pain that she could have been looking at how to kill someone for all he cared. They'd moved him around so much and bumped his leg that he was nearly sick with the pain of it.

"Hang on, Thad. They're going to bring you something for pain." He said that he couldn't leave his sisters. Mr. Gibb smiled at him. "I won't leave them. Nor you. You just let them give you something for the pain then you'll be able to rest. They're going to take you up to surgery in a few minutes to clean up that wound and make sure that the infection is taken care of. You're going to be just fine. I promise you."

He didn't want to question him about how he was going to make that happen. But he was worried. As soon as the nurse came in, she said that she was going to start an IV on him and he'd get something for the pain. Almost as soon as she told him he was going to feel a pinch, it was all over his body, this feeling of being without pain. Then she told him that he was going to feel drowsy but not to fight it. Thad thought that it was the most amazing thing in the world when she told him to close his eyes.

When he woke up, he was in a different room. There were three beds in the room, his sisters were in them sleeping and a big chair. He looked around the room, not entirely sure how he'd gotten in here, when he saw Mr. Gibb sitting in the chair next to his bed.

"I can talk to you like this if you want. Belle told me that you guys can talk to each other through a link as well. This way, we won't wake them. They're just as exhausted as you are." Thad asked him how he'd gotten in here. *"Your surgery went fine. You're on the mend now, and once the infection is out of your body, they'll send us home. The doctor said you'd need to stay here for a couple of days before he was ready to release you because of the infection. But you're going to be just fine."*

Again, the urge to cry rolled over him. Mr. Gibb sat up in the chair more and took his hand into his. He told him he was all right to be brave sometimes, but now he only needed to get well.

"Your mom is doing better, too. They removed the bullets, and she's resting. In the morning, they're going to put her into a room where you guys can go and see her. She might not be awake fully, but she'll be here for a few more days longer than you will be." He asked where they were going to be staying. *"I have a big house on*

my family's land that you and your sisters will be able to go to. My family lives on a mountain that has been in our family for generations. I do want to talk to you about something. Do you know what a shifter is?"

"Yes." He looked at the big man. "You're one, aren't you? All of your family – that's why Mr. Mark said you were all magical. You're a shifter, too. That means that you're super strong, doesn't it?"

"Yes, it does. I'm a bear. A black bear. All of my brothers are. The reason that I'm asking you about this is that your mom is my mate. Do you know what that means?" He nodded, then shook his head. "She and I are like husband and wife. But I want you to know that I won't ever harm her. Nor will I allow someone else to hurt her, either. My entire family will protect you all with their lives. And as far as I'm concerned, you three are my children, and I will die before I let anyone or anything hurt you."

"Do you think that someone will – my uncle, Dave? He'll come after us again, won't he? He thinks that we should belong to him. He said that mom is really stupid and won't raise us right. He just wants what we can do. He scares us, Mr. Gibb." Mr. Gibb nodded. Then told him what his uncle had been thinking about for the last several weeks. "He won't give up until he gets killed or he kills one of us. You think he'll be like that with Mom, too? Killing her off even though she's his little sister?"

"He nearly did it when he shot her today. But it's all about money, Especially free money coming to him with you guys helping will make everyone greedy. Greedy men and women will go to great links, even killing someone who is related to them to get what they think they need or deserve. I want you to know that I'd never ask you to do that for me. No one else will, either. I know I keep saying this. But I do promise you." Thad said that for helping them with keeping them safe, they'd do that for him. No problem. "I wouldn't ask you. I have a great deal of money, Thad. And in saying that, you and your family do as well. If Dave won every horse race from now until he's dead, he'd not have nearly as much money as I do. I'm a very wealthy man. As are all my brothers and their families. We don't need to cheat to have more. We have plenty enough as it is."

"Mom said we don't have two pennies to rub together." He smiled at him and told him that she wouldn't have to worry about that anymore. "You don't know my mom. She worries about everything. Even before we started running, we had some money. But she'd worry about a rainy day coming around. Sheesh, women are strange, don't you think?"

"I'm not going to answer that. If your mom were to hear us talking about her like this, she'd brain us both, I think." Thad laughed. It felt good. Also like a weight as big as him had been taken off him. *"All right, buddy. You need to get some rest. We're all going to be staying here until you can go home with us. My sisters-in-law are taking care that your rooms are set up nicely, and you have clothing to wear for the next few days. After that, we'll be playing it by ear until your mom is awake."*

Thad was asked if he wanted pain meds from the nurse when she came in. It was Belle who answered for him that he did. Then she and Maria climbed into the bed with him, and they snuggled up. Like they'd been doing since this nightmare began. Thad had never been so happy about having someone looking over them as he was right now. He thought they might be all right with Mr. Gibb and his brothers.

Chapter 2

Dave didn't mind being in the jail cell. So far, he'd been able to get his wounds taken care of and a couple of nice meals. They weren't anything that he would have ordered for himself, but they filled the void until he got out of there. And he would, too. It was just a matter of time. Also, it afforded him time to plot and plan the demise of Maddy.

What had gotten him arrested this time was while he'd been trying to find a way to kill his sister, he'd decided that he'd pull a fire alarm at the hospital where she'd been at. That was, in part, why he was currently sitting in a cell. But some stupid bitch calling herself a big witch or something had fucked that over for him. Every single time—no matter where it was either—that he touched the alarm, he'd be zapped across the room where he'd hit his head. He still had a headache, but at least the cops were making sure that he wasn't in too much pain.

Dave laid back on his cot and thought about the money that he'd won by just having the brats for a few hours. The little shits were special, and he had planned on using them until they were used up. The race tracks were his, he'd thought. Every time he placed a bet, he'd win. Even on the other side bets that he'd do with other people. Like the time that the horses came in. Christ, he'd been rolling in the dough.

But it was all gone now. Every last penny was spent because he never dreamed that someone would come and take his meal ticket from him. Especially his sister. He thought for sure she'd not miss them at all. They were whiney little fuckers. However, she went and called the police on him. Damned fucking bitch. It didn't even last him a week with all the things that he'd needed to buy and take care of.

Locking the kids in the basement with just enough food and water to keep them living, he'd gone out to dinner with a bunch of his buddies — him buying, of course. Only to come home to find that not only were they not in the basement anymore but that the police had been waiting on him. Christ, it had taken some fast talking and what was left of his cash to get out of that one.

Then he'd lost his sister, too. Maddy wasn't all that smart. He'd never thought so. At least she'd been able to birth some special kids. But she was stupid as the day was long with them kids being around her all the time. She'd had a great money maker right there in her possession — three of them, as a matter of fact, and she never once used them. They could have been the richest people in the whole of the world, and she was washing dishes for a living. If that wasn't bad enough, she had her kids looking in dumpsters for shit to eat, too. Christ, she really was about the dumbest person alive.

"Mr. Farley, you have a visitor. They want to have a meeting with you in a room here on the premises. Are you all right with that?" He asked who it was. "You want me to send them home, or do you want to talk to them? I'm to keep you informed, not wipe your nose when you need it."

He didn't know where this man's hostility was coming from. Up until just now, they'd been nice to him. Telling the officer that he'd meet the person in a room, he was told to stand back from the bars while he opened the door. As it turned out, he was also waiting for four more officers to come down the hall, too. Something was off, and he wasn't sure what was going on. But he knew that he'd find out.

Once he was in the little room, he was handcuffed, something that he'd not been before and also cuffed to the table and floor. The table, he noticed, was screwed down, and he'd bet anything that even if he had the strength of fifty men, he'd not be able to move it. Dave was still thinking about it when four men in suits came into the room with him.

"Mr. David Winslow Farley, I presume?" He said that was him. "Good. My name is Federal Officer Jacob Winchester. I'm here to make you aware of the things that are going on with your case. You are being recorded with a camera that is pointed directly at you. Also, each of us here has a camera on us that not only has visual but audio as well. You will sign this paperwork that states that you've been made aware of these things." He signed his name just where he was told.

The man whipped the paperwork out from under his hand and looked it over. Like he'd not ever seen it before. When he seemed satisfied, he had one of the other men with him sign, too. Then he put it in a briefcase that he'd brought in with him. When he just sat there. Dave decided he had a few questions of his own to ask.

"What case is this about? If this is about my sister's kids, I want you to know that I'm going to be taking them from her again. They have something that I want. And even if I have to kill her, I'll do it to get them." He'd forgotten that the big witch had told him that he wouldn't be able to lie anymore to anyone, so he clamped his mouth tightly shut. The man, Winchester, just stared at him.

"You want to tell me what it is you think that they owe you? They're only ten years old, Mr. Farley. I doubt that they would be owing you money." Dave shook his head. Hard enough that it hurt. "Oh, why not? This could be fun for us. I mean…you know what, I'm going to ask you questions, and if I have to get Amelia here to make you talk, I will. What do you think the kids owe you? You'll tell me now."

He fought hard on not opening his mouth. His jaws were hurting; he had them clinched so badly. But once he started talking, because really, he'd not had a choice, he began telling him just what he thought the kids owed him.

"They have this freaky ability that I don't understand. But I do know that I can use it to make myself rich as Midas. And I want that, too. To be the richest man in the world. They made me a wad of cash before, but I spent it stupidly. I know that now. Please? Please don't ask me anything else. I beg of you. I can't lie anymore." Instead of letting him go back to his cell and forget about this, the officer asked him how that worked with the brats. Crying now, he answered him. "They can see which horse is going to win and by how much, even down to the second. I tried them on a little bit of lottery numbers, too, and they got them all, even the extra ones. I couldn't get them to tell me the big lottery numbers. The little fuckers. I'll get them to do that even if I have to kill one of them to make them. They'll see things my way once I start hurting the others. You watch—don't do this to me. This isn't right at all. It's not fair."

"Like we care what you think is fair or not. Now. We're getting somewhere now. Why did you kill your parents?" The Fed actually smiled at him. "You're going to be able to solve a lot of open cases for us if I don't miss my bet. I'm going to have to thank Agent Cross for her help on this."

They continued to ask him about names of the dead that he'd not thought about for decades. His parents were just the first of many that he'd been told had been exhumed and were right now being tested for DNA and fingerprints. He'd even gone so far as the tell the man where the murder weapons were and how he'd disposed of the few things that were easy to burn up. He was hoarse by the time they called it a day. Then they told him that they'd be back tomorrow.

"Also, your accommodations will be different, too, starting tonight. You will be in a different cell as well as have a Federal Officer in front of it at all times. Don't expect to have special meals brought in for you, but you'll eat what we give you. Also, you'll do this without complaint. There are other things that are going to happen to you, Mr. Farley, and we'll get to those later." As the man was packing up the things that he'd brought in with him, he looked at the other agents with him. "I think this calls for a celebration. We'll find us a good steak house and have the works. The President will be very pleased with the day's events."

He was nearly dragged back to his new cell. And it was just as he said, too. Not only did his 'accommodations' change in that he had a smaller cell as well as no window now, but he also didn't have as many blankets as he'd had before. Just a thin one that he could literally see through. Lying in his bed, he thought of the big witch. Then, there was something tickling at his head, and she spoke to him again. The bitch.

"It's grand witch, you idiot, not big." Dave asked her why she was doing this to him. *"Because you're a bad person and did this to yourself. Besides, you've no idea how much better the kids are sleeping knowing that you're not going to be trying to kill them anymore. Oh, even though you didn't ask, Maddy is doing well too. She's weak, of course, but healing more and more daily. Aren't you thrilled about that?"*

"No, I am not. She should be dead. Why do I have a feeling that you had something to do with that, too? You did it, didn't you? Like you make me tell the truth all the time. You gave her some of your mojo, and now she's going to live forever." Witchy told him that he was correct on both. *"Both? What are you talking about?"*

"She's going to live forever. So are the kids. Even if you were to get out right now and be given free access to them, you'd not be able to do much more than to piss off a sleuth of bears. One of them being her new mate." He asked her what that meant. The sleuth and mate shit meant. *"Sleuth means a group of bears. There are a lot of them, too. And just pissed off enough at you to do you great harm. Mate? Well, like we explained it to the children,*

they're man and wife. You'll also be happy to know that with her being mated to a bear, a black one if you're at all curious, it's made them both much stronger than they were before. Gibb is about the sweetest man to those little children. They're happy — "

"I don't care how fucking happy they are. I want them to come here and get me out of here." She said that no one was going to do that for him, even if they could. "Of course they can. Just come on down here, tell them that I didn't hurt none of them. Even have dumbass Maddy tell them that I didn't pull the trigger on her and I'll take her kids. She owes me that much for not dying when I shot her. The stupid bitch. You too. You both should be dead."

"Okay, let's go over today's events, shall we? You've been sitting with four federal agents for the last several hours, is that right?" He asked her what that had to do with anything. "I'd think plenty since you confessed to over three dozen murders, including the attempted murder of your other sister. Then there is the confession of you killing off a high-profile federal attorney. That alone will get you a lot of years tacked onto the several lifetimes that you're going to serve now."

"Nobody can serve more than one lifetime. Everyone knows that. It's just asinine that they said that someone is *going to be serving five life sentences. You can't. So that's not going to work. And as for me confessing to killing people, I'm going to tell them that some grand witch made me not be able to lie. That'll get me something."*

"Yes, locked up. Do you think that anyone is going to believe that there is a witch around? No. Not many. And even those that might believe, they're going to keep their mouth shut in the event that said witch came after them." Her laughter grated on his nerves, making his head ache all the more. *"Poor Dave. He's going to go to federal prison for a very long time, and he won't ever get to abuse or use people again. I'm sure a lot of people are going to have a party in your name, too."*

"We'll just see about that, won't we? I got this in the bag." There were times when he didn't understand a single word that came out of his mouth. Ignoring her laughing at him, he started to speak again. Then he thought of a bribe. *"I'll tell you what. I'll not give you a single penny of the money that I'll promise you if you get me out of here."* He thought about what he said. *"Damn it, woman. It's getting old having to tell the truth all the time. I demand that you take that shit away from me. A man like me can't be telling the truth all the time. I'll get myself killed if I keep doing this."*

"One less prick around if that were to happen. No,

you're going to be away forever, Dave. And people all around will be happy as a bug in a rug." She laughed again, and he wanted to scream at her. *"Tomorrow will be a big day for you. You need to be on your best behavior, or you might not make it to prison at all."*

"What's that supposed to mean? Are you saying that there is a chance that I can get out of this? Is that it?" Her laughter was fading away, and he was screaming at her out loud now to tell him what she was talking about. "Come back here. You hear me? I said to come back here and explain to me what you meant. Am I getting—"

"Shut your mouth, or I'll shut it for you." He'd forgotten about the guard. Telling him that he wasn't sorry about yelling made the man growl at him. Fucker was more than likely one of them shifter things. They were taking over the world.

Lying down on his cot, he realized that his mattress wasn't nearly as soft as it had been. Not that it was all that comfy, but this one was thin as a sheet and no bigger than the bed. Rolling over, Dave was going to figure out how she meant that he wasn't getting out. He would, by god, too. And kill the lot of them.

~*~

Maddy had been home from the hospital for two days now, and she was about as bored as she'd ever been. The kids were going to school during the day, which left her with her own thoughts. Mostly, those centered around Gibb Cross and what she'd been finding out about him. And it seemed that everyone had a tidbit about the handsome man, too. Looking up when someone said her name, she glared at the bane of her existence right now.

"Where have you been?" Gibb laughed and told her that he'd told her he was taking the kids to school when they left. "Oh. You said you'd be right back. What time is it?"

"Just after nine. It takes a little bit to get to the Indian school. I also told you that." He sat down across from her wheelchair. "Why are you in a mood now? I mean, you've been in a terrible mood since you woke up."

"I'm not in a terrible mood." He reminded her that she'd made Belle cry this morning. "I told her that I was sorry. I'm just in pain."

She wasn't, and she was sure that he knew it. The only reason that she was in the wheelchair right now was because she'd gotten a little dizzy when thinking about how she should be dead. Looking away from Gibb, she decided that it was time she told him what was going on. Or at least a bit of it.

"I'm broke. More than that…I guess you would know that, too. The kids told you that as well." He said that he knew she had been broke. Then told her that they had but she wasn't any longer. She looked at him. "What are you going to do? Hand over control of all your money? Give me credit cards that have no limit on them and tell me to spend what I want?"

When he stood up, she nearly rolled away from him. Taking her hand into his, he kissed her palm, then laid a stack of credit cards in her palm before returning to the seat. He didn't say anything, but she did look at the names on the cards.

"These are in my name. With Cross on them. I'm not a Cross." He said that he was aware of that, but he didn't want her to have any trouble using them when she wanted. "Why would I have trouble? Because you'd cause it?"

"No." He laughed a little, but she knew that he was forcing himself to be civil to her. "I don't want to cause you any trouble. You seem to be doing that all on your own. Did you actually tell the children not to get too close to my family because you weren't going to be staying? Thad cried for an hour before I was able to get him to go to sleep last night. Maria said she wasn't going to talk to you ever again if you made her leave here. I didn't tell them to say that, but they're upset with you. So am I if you want to know the truth."

"You'll toss us aside when Dave gives you enough money to take them from you." She knew that as soon as she said it, she'd hurt him. Deeply too. "I'm sorry."

"I could tell you that it's all right, but it's not. You've been a real bitch since yesterday. I didn't do anything to you but to keep your children safe and make sure that they were able to see you while in the hospital. You've been rude, mean and a royal pain in the ass to everyone. I'm just glad that my grandparents aren't here so that you'd be picking at them as well." He stood up this time, and she could see the anger around him. "I'm going to go outside for a spell. I don't know when I'll see you again. But if you want something, you need only to reach out to anyone but me. I will bring the kids home from school to be with you. Until then, there is staff here." He started for the doorway before stopping and turning back to her. "I don't want nor need Dave's money. Even if he had any, which he doesn't. We have plenty enough as it is. You enjoy your day. Or not. Right now, I don't care what you do."

The door slamming had her angry. Then just as she realized that she didn't have any reason whatsoever to be pissed off, she burst into tears. She really didn't know what was wrong with her. Every little thing pissed her off. Even good things like having the kids well taken care of and happy. Well, they'd been happy until last night.

She didn't know what had possessed her to tell them that they couldn't stay here. There was no reason for her to have said that. No one had hurt them. Nor had they been in her face about things. When Sunny had come over last night and told her how things were progressing with Dave and his prison sentence, she'd pissed her off too. Not only did she not tell her off, which is what Maddy thought she wanted to, but she'd left after telling the kids how much she loved being around them.

"You going to get your head out of your ass and start figuring out how good you have it?" She asked who she was speaking to. *"Jamie. I'm mate to Mark, the oldest. I just ran into Gibb. I don't think I've ever seen him that mad before. I knew it had to be you who did it. He said he was going to talk to you this morning while the kids were*

at school. I'm assuming that it didn't go as he planned."

"I was rude to him. Mean, too, he told me." She asked if she had been. *"Yes. I don't know what's wrong with me."*

"Did you happen to tell him that? I'm sure that he would have answered the question that has been going on in your head for the last few days. I can answer it for you. He won't ever ask the kids for anything like your own brother did. Nor will he harm them in any way. I know that for a fact." Jamie didn't say anything for a few seconds, then laughed. *"I see. You know that as well. He's probably one of the nicest men that I've ever met. All the Cross men are. They're hurting, too, by the way. Their grandda was killed a few days before you were shot, and then their granny, unable to live without him, passed away the same night. Those two raised those men when their mother wanted nothing to do with them."*

"Thad told me." She said that the kids were a good balm for all of them. *"They are for me as well. However, I made them cry."*

"I know that. Everyone does. Thad went to Gibb for comfort, and his brothers were with him. Then Maria and Belle, who I dearly love, by the way, came to the house and cried, too. You're batting a thousand if you ask me. I believe the only person that you've not pissed off is your cook.

And she's trying hard to please you so she doesn't lose her job. She likes having money in the bank while raising ten children, five of which aren't even hers." Maddy asked why she was raising five children not her own. *"Her little sister was killed last summer while out and about as her lioness. She was killed when some jack assed men thought it would be fun to hunt on National land. They're going to prison for killing a lion when, in actuality, they killed a woman who was all alone but for her children and sister."*

    "Does that — would you please come here? I don't mind talking to you, but I'd like to have the company. Also, the help. I've messed up. A great deal." Jamie said that she had. With the entire family. *"You don't cut any slack, do you? I mean, I'm trying here. Can't you give me something for that?"*

    "No. I doubt that anyone will until you make Gibb happy. No, not happy but not pissed. You did something that I didn't think was possible. You hurt his heart. It had been so full when he found out that not only did he have a mate but three children to raise as his own, too. And he's been doing a fucking fantastic job about it as well. Not only do the kids have everything that they need in the way of making that place a home, but they're happy and healthy. Or they were." Maddy's heart hurt, too. Because she

didn't know how to acknowledge that someone was taking better care of her family than she had. *"Don't. Don't think that. You're all alive, aren't you?"*

"Barely." She looked around the living room. *"I just noticed that this place is nearly devoid of furniture. Why is that? Please tell me that he didn't just purchase this house for the four of us."*

"No. He's owned it for some time, I guess. All of them have a house. Mark and I live in the homestead. It's been upgraded. While the crew was here, Gibb had a construction crew come out and add onto his home and upgrade the things that he'd started and not finished. All the homes up here have been taken care of." She could feel Jamie speaking to someone else. While she didn't know why she did, she also knew that she was on the phone. *"I'm on my way over there. So are Sunny and Amelia. Don't piss us off."*

Maddy told her that she'd try her best not to. Getting up, she made her way to the kitchen. The cook, she didn't know her name, was making bread, something that she knew her kids loved more than anything. Asking her name and if she could have some tea and cookies for when the other women came over, Kerry told her that she'd baked some this morning for the kids, but she'd bring things right out.

By the time the other women were in the living room, Maddy was feeling overwhelmed again. It was Sunny who helped her navigate her way around her anxiety, and once she started feeling better, they sat down to talk. Knowing that none of them would sugarcoat things, she got right down to business with what she wanted answers on. They'd either help or kill her, and right now, she was thinking that they'd gladly hurt her over helping her.

"I've been on the run for nearly two years now. Since my kids just turned eight. I need help. I've not been able to let others help me and be able to depend on them since they were born. Their father knocked the crap out of me three days after they were born, and I've been on my own since." Amelia told her that she was no longer alone. "I know that in my head. But my heart is having a really hard time here. Can you help me?"

Chapter 3

Gibb was waiting in line to pick up the kids. He saw Belle first, then the other two as they came out of the building. Smiling, he knew that this was just what he needed to have his day end on a better note. But the closer they got to his car, he could see that they were very upset and they needed him.

Pulling out of the line, he parked his car and went to them. Belle, usually the one who would be the most vocal about things, asked him to hold her. Picking her up, she buried her face in the crook of his neck and cried. Thad looked as pissed off as he'd been this morning. Maria was holding onto her sister's backpack and steaming, too. He got down to their level while still holding his daughter.

"What's happened?" Thad looked back at the school, and he saw three teachers coming his way. "Did you guys want me to take care of this or go and get your mom? I'm all right with whatever you decide."

"You, please. Mom is...she might hurt somebody. And then we'd all be in more trouble." He nodded, barely holding onto his laughter at the face that Thad had made talking about his mom. "But I promise you, Gibb. We didn't do what they're going to tell you we did. I swear."

All three of them nodded, even Belle. When the principal caught up with the teachers, he was asked to come into the office. That the kids would be all right playing in the yard. He said no, they'd be with him. Instead of arguing, they all went into the school again.

"Apparently, Sir, I'm to understand that your children have been causing trouble." Gibb sat down, and the kids surrounded him. Holding their hands as best he could, he didn't comment on what Mr. Walkinghorse, the principal, said to him.

"Officer Cross, when we said that we'd take them into our system, you said that they were good kids. But I've heard today that they cheat on tests. The three of them are in it together. I apologize for not having all the details as yet, but their teacher is here to explain."

"And you can prove this, I'm assuming?" Instead of talking, he handed him three tests. After looking them over, he smiled. "Because they have the same wording for each answer, you're accusing them of cheating. I know for a fact that they're not even in the same room. Nor do they have lunch at the same time. Tell me how you think they're cheating. Also, so you know, when we were studying for this test last night, we did the studying as a team. If I had been asked to answer those questions, I would have worded it the same way, too. Because that's the way that we studied it. Now that you have all the facts on my end, I'm assuming that you've asked the kids to give you their version."

"They do have the same answers." Gibb said nothing to Ms. Jonas. He thought that she was Belle's teacher. "Well, don't you think that's a little suspicious? I do."

"I can't help that you have a suspicious mind, Ms. Jonas. But they didn't cheat. They couldn't have. Unless, of course, you know how it happened. Because with the circumstances being what they are, it would have been impossible for them to have done it. Not to mention, they told you they'd not. That right there is proof enough for me."

"She said that they cheated. That they had copied off of each other. I didn't know they were in different rooms. This is making less sense than it did when she told me about it. However, I did want to get you in on this from the start *if* there is a problem." Mr. Walkinghorse looked at Ms. Jonas. "You started this. Tell them what reason you'd have to say that three kids in different classes living in the same home would be able to cheat. I'd like an answer to that myself. And so you're aware, Ms. Jonas, I'm well aware of your talking the other two teachers into saying the same thing." Becca Jewel, Thad's teacher, spoke up then.

"I don't believe it either, sir. I'm only here to tell you that I think it's wrong that you've separated these kids from each other. I've heard about what they've been through, and separating them now isn't doing any of them any good. They're great kids, all three of them. And they couldn't have a better stepfather than Gibb Cross here." Mrs. Jewel laid down a sheet of paper. "That's my resignation, Mr. Walkinghorse. If Debra stays here, I'm not going to. She's nothing but trouble. And I don't want to be dragged into her drama anymore. She goes, or I do. That's all there is to it."

Two other teachers told him the same thing. That if Ms. Jonas stayed, they were gone. Gibb had a feeling too that by the end of tomorrow, the school would be down all the teachers but Debra, if this didn't end as he hoped it would. He asked if his kids were going to get an apology. Everyone turned and looked at Debra.

"From me? No. Not on your life. They cheated, and I know they did. I don't know how, but they did it." She looked at the kids, and Belle lifted her chin up in defiance. Gibb couldn't fault her for that. "That one there is the ring leader. She's forever mouthing off."

"She's wrong. All the time, she says the wrong things. Like she told the class that white people were here first and that having Indians around was a bad example to the world. Also, she can't add right. When we take a test, she marks my papers wrong, and I get a bad grade. I know how to add things up." Gibb asked Belle if she had one of her papers that the teacher had marked wrong. As she was digging into her pack, she looked up at him. "You believe me. You really do."

"I really do. Show me what she's been doing to you, honey." She handed him a stack of papers.

All of them had a fat red F on them. Sorting through them, he could see that just the top three alone were all right and should have been marked with an A. "What is this? Even I can tell that she's gotten these all correct. What are you doing to my daughter?"

"I don't like her. Nor those red skins either." Gibb couldn't believe that she'd just said that. The room was deathly silent. Finally, Gibb looked at Mr. Walkinghorse. "Yes, I said it. The red skins. I'd not be teaching here at all if not for the fact that the pay is better and there are a lot of perks."

Mr. Walkinghorse looked at him before speaking. He could see that the man was both shocked and embarrassed. He looked at him with a tight smile.

"Gibb, sir. Why don't you take your children home with you? I'll handle this from now on. And Ms. Belle, child, if you could give me your papers, I'll make sure that they're marked correctly." Debra said that she'd not count them toward her grade then. He turned on the woman in a second. "Sit down and shut the hell up. I've had enough of you today."

He was ushering the kids out to the car when he realized something that hadn't occurred to him before. Walkinghorse was a shifter. A horse shifter.

Not that it mattered. He was a good man and someone that had won his respect today. He only hoped that the man would take care that Debra wasn't employed there anymore.

As soon as the kids were buckled into their seats, he decided that they'd been roughed up enough for one day and told them they were going to get ice cream. That had the response that he had hoped it would. There were two places that he knew of on this side of the mountains that he could take them to. They were still deciding on what they wanted when he reached out to Maddy.

"I have the kids. I'm sure that they'll tell you about their day when they get there. I want you to know that they've come out on top from a terrible teacher. She accused them of cheating." She didn't ask if they had, for which he was glad. *"I'm taking them to get ice cream. Then, when I bring them home, someone is going to have to talk to them about the things that the teacher said to them."*

"I think that they deserve ice cream as well. If I were with you, I'd have one as well. The kids, they might well be able to communicate with each other, but they would never cheat. I'm assuming you knew that, too." He said that he did. And then thanked her for agreeing with him. *"I've had a long talk with the women in this family.*

I'm sorry for the way that I treated you this morning. I'm overwhelmed. Not just a little, either. Also, terrified that you might toss us aside. I never gave you a chance for anything, and I'm profoundly sorry for that."

"*Thank you for that. I know you've been through a great deal, but none of us would ever harm you."* She said that she knew that as well but that she really was sorry. "*The kids and I will be home soon. They deserve ice cream, as you said. They've been having a rough time at school and never said anything. I need to talk to them about that — we need to talk to them about that, too. That we can't fix things if they don't tell us about them."*

"*I think they, too, are slightly overwhelmed. And I didn't help matters by being a bitch."* Gibb wisely kept his mouth shut. Then she laughed. "*I guess that's putting me in my place. Thank you for not agreeing or disagreeing with me. I think I needed that as well. And yes, we need to talk to them about a lot of stuff. Thank you for taking care of them."*

"*It's been my pleasure."* He pulled up in front of the ice cream parlor and told Maddy that they'd be home in about an hour. "All right, kiddos, let's go and ruin our dinner before your mom tells me that you can't do this all the time."

They didn't overindulge. He was sure that as

a child, as well as most kids, he would have ordered the biggest thing on the menu. But all they did was order a dish of ice cream each and decided to share with each other. They each got a different flavor, including him and four spoons. It was the most enjoyable time he'd ever had, just having a bowl of ice cream.

"Gibb. Me and the others have been talking." He asked Thad about what. "I'm getting to that. Did you know that we call all your brothers Uncle and their wives, who we love, too, Aunt?"

"I did. I think you've made them very proud of that title, too. Mark told me he'd never been an uncle before and quite enjoyed being called one." Thad said that was what he'd told them the same thing. Belle said she'd never been an aunt before, either. "If my brothers have children with their wives or more kids come along to the family like you guys did for me, then you'll be cousins. Have you ever been one of those before?"

"Nope." Thad asked Belle to let him talk. "Oh, go on with you then. You always have to lead up to something. Just say it. I know that I do when I gots something to say."

"Everyone knows that. That's why I'm asking

you to let me ask him if we can call him dad or not." It took Gibb a moment to realize what Thad had said. Pulling over, he turned in the seat and looked at the three of them. "Well, I guess you know. Can we? Call you Dad now? We've never had one of those, either. I mean, I guess we did, but he's in prison and not ever coming out. But it sure would be wonderful if we could call you Dad."

"I'd be honored to be called your dad." When they unbuckled and climbed over the seat to get to him, Gibb was sure that he could have taken on the entire mountain of black bears and didn't even care if he came out on the top or bottom. He was about as high as he could be right now. After several more hugs and them calling him dad over and over, he told them that their mom was expecting them. Getting another hug, he watched them buckle in, and he then did the same for himself.

Gibb was never going to be the same after today. He was someone's dad. Three someone's. His heart was full, his life going well, and he had lifetimes of being with these kids and any more that came into his life.

Pulling into the drive, he was glad to see their mom on the front porch. There were delivery trucks there, too, and she was directing them, he thought. Gibb had forgotten about the kids' furniture being delivered today and should have warned her. They all three had beds from the large barn out in the back of the land, but dressers and other things, like homework desks, hadn't been there for them. However, as he got closer to her, he could tell that she had a handle on things.

"My goodness. It's been a long time since we've all had new furniture." The kids seemed to be a little standoffish with their mom at first, but they soon realized that she was all right again. He'd not realized until then that they'd been a little afraid of her when she'd been upset. Hugging them, she told them that it would be all week putting things together. "Unless you guys can convince your uncles and aunts to come over and help. We'll even have a cookout together if they agree. What do you think?"

"They're coming now." Belle went into the house and came back out to look up at her momma. "Are you all better now? You're not going to tell us again that we're not to love it here, are you? I just called Gibb here, Dad. I don't want you to have to take that away from us. Do you?"

Maddy looked at him and smiled while

speaking to her kids. "No. I'm glad that you've decided that he could be your dad. I don't think that you could do any better than him. But you guys go in and change, and we'll get the rest of the truck unloaded. All right?" Ten minutes later, his brothers showed up in full force.

~*~

"So what did they do with her? I'm assuming— well, hoping that she's been fired." Gibb told her that he'd not heard anything, but that didn't mean much. "Yes, I suppose they'd not put it out there that they had a bigot working for them. And that she had to be terminated. Why did you pick that particular school?"

"I've known about the school since I was a kid. I'd never heard anything bad about it. So when I went looking for a place where the kids would be safe, I enrolled them there. Mr. Walkinghorse was all right with them being temporary in the event that you wished to put them someplace else. But I do think that they're having a good time and they seem to love it there. Also, they're all three in the same class now. I never agreed with them being separated either." Maddy told Gibb that she was glad they were together, too. "The first couple of nights here, we only had a couple of air mattresses for them to sleep on. They all huddled in the same room, so I didn't rush to get their beds set up. Then, one afternoon, I was with Mark and Barron out at the big barn when they joined us. The first thing that they fell in love with was the big beds. The girls loved the bunk beds. I think that I had a set in my room, and so did Mark. Thad said that he wanted a bigger bed so he could spread out when he wanted to. I think it had more to do with them all getting into his bed after I put them to bed. However, now, they all sleep in their own rooms."

"When they were little, we only had a two-bedroom place. They all three shared the same room. It wasn't so bad back then. But it was difficult as they got older. Especially since their personalities are so different. I have to admit, Maria was the one who was forever backward when they were together. Now, she is out there just as much as they are. I'm so glad for that."

Maddy pulled the stuff out of the cabinet to make pancakes for the kids for breakfast before they left for school. Gibb told her that they'd not eat that. It was on the tip of her tongue to tell him that she knew the kids better than he did when he spoke while making their lunches.

"When they first got here, the cook asked them what they wanted to eat. All three of them said that they never wanted to eat another pancake as long as they lived. Thad told me that it was about the only thing they had to eat while you were working, and they got sick of it." He looked up at her and smiled. "They also don't want to have sandwiches. Maria told me that she and the others got sick on some meat that they'd found and they'd not been able to eat it since. I've tried to get them to branch out on subs, and so far, that's working. But I don't know how to change up pancakes for them to ever eat again."

"We did have a lot of pancake meals while on the run." She thought about what else they'd eaten a great deal of while they'd been homeless. "Sometimes, I'd take a little of my check and get them a treat. They never wanted a candy bar or anything like that. And they never had soda before, either. Their idea of a treat was to have ranch dressing and carrots. I think they might still like that."

"They do. Thad, not as much as the girls, but he calls it girly food. I have no idea where he might have gotten that from. But I did take them out to the garden that my grandma had before she passed.

We were able to find a few carrots that had been left behind. You should have seen their faces when they tasted them. They're nothing at all like the ones you get from the store." Gibb laughed. "Next year, we're going to grow a lot of fresh vegetables. Even for being bears, we eat a lot of fresh when we have it."

"Do you eat a lot of meat? I mean, large qualities of it?" He said no more than a human would, he supposed. "I'm not much of a red meat fan. I can eat it, but it's not my go-to comfort food. I do love seafood and fish, however."

For the last few days, they'd been hanging out together and learning things about each other. She knew a good deal more about him than she thought he did her simply because the kids would tell her something that they learned about him. She, too, had been getting information and tidbits here and there from the family, too. It was fun getting to know Gibb and his family. When the kids, dressed for school, joined them in the kitchen, she had made them eggs and sausage with toast.

"Momma, did you remember about the class project for next week. We gave you a supply list, remember?" Maddy told Belle that she was going into town today to get it. "Goody. Thad and Maria and I aren't allowed to work on the project together. The teacher wants us to get to know the others in the class, so she let us get into other groups. I have three new friends."

"That's wonderful news, honey. Are you enjoying your classes then?" Thad told her that he was having trouble with his math, but his Aunt Sunny was helping him with it. "I'm very happy that you guys have all your aunts and uncles, but don't bother them too much. They all have jobs to do, too. Remember that."

"I do. And I told Aunt Sunny that if she was busy, she could tell me that. She said that if she had a problem with me coming to her for help, then she needs to be knocked on her butt. Only she didn't say butt. She's really funny when she tries not to cruse around us. Her face gets all purple. She went to anger management school for a while, she told us. I think she's so funny."

Maddy glanced at Gibb when she heard that Sunny had gone to anger classes. He explained the story behind her having to go. Apparently, someone thought that she was too caustic when telling them that they'd done something wrong. As it turned out, Sunny had been right and the other person wrong.

But that she finished the class as she had really enjoyed it.

"She's all right now. I think she has been all along." Nodding, she fried another egg for Belle when she asked. Gibb finished up with their lunches and sat down to continue the story. "She's been working on some projects for the president. And when she's finished with those, she said she's going to retire. I don't think she will. She's not only good at her job, but she enjoys it too. What is it you did for a living?"

The question caught her off guard a little, and she had to think. After telling him that she really didn't have a talent but had been working in a factory, he smiled at her. It was enough to melt through her heart, and she turned her back. Christ, the man was just too handsome and sweet at times.

"There aren't any factory jobs around here. However, if you want to work, I'm sure that we can find you something that you might enjoy. But as I told you last night, there isn't any reason for you to have to work." She told him that she wanted to do something or she'd be bored. "I understand that very well. Have you been to the Cross Shoppe? Granny mostly ran it. We all put our things in it. We've been looking for someone to run it for us. If you think that is something that you might enjoy, I can take you there to have a look around. Also, while we're in town, we need to look at a car for you."

"I used to have a car. But I don't know what happened to it. We also had a nice home that we rented, that I don't know what happened to that either." She thought of some of the things that had been left behind when Dave had come after them. "I'm sure that whatever was there has been trashed by now. It's been a while."

"I can have one of the women look into that for you if you remember the address. I don't know how much luck they'll have, but it's worth a shot." She told him that she'd give it to him later. "All right. You guys ready to head out? Mom is taking you in today. I have some work to do with the gardens."

She was sort of nervous about driving into town. Just from her working around here for the last month, she knew that the congestion on the streets was horrific and there were too many people around. But she had told Gibb that she'd do it, and she was determined to make it work.

As soon as the kids were buckled into the back seat of his car, she started it up. So far, so good. Just as she was ready to pull down out of the driveway,

Gibb came out of his building toward them. He was holding his cell phone to his ear, and she wondered what had happened now.

"It's the police station. They want to talk to you." She took the phone from him, and he told her to get in on the other side, and he'd take them into town now. As she braced herself for whatever they wanted, Gibb was telling the kids that he had their lists of lunch treats as well as the projects list.

"I'm sorry to bother you, Mrs. Cross, but Mr. Farley has been asking to see you. Demanding, really, but I told him that I'd give you a call. I don't know what he might want; he's going to be transferred to a federal prison in the morning, and he wants to see you before he goes. If you don't want to come in, I can surely understand that." The man laughed a little. "I promise you that you'll be as safe as you are at your home there with Gibb. Or any of the Cross men. There is a guard on him all the time now, and he'll be behind bars, too. That is if you decide to come in."

She nearly told the man that she never wanted to see the man again. That she had had enough of him over the last eight years of having to keep on the run with three kids. Then she thought of something else. He was the one behind bars, not her. If she saw him, then she could walk away freely. He never would be again.

"Do I need to give you a time to come in?" He said that if she could make it around noonish, that would help them out a bit. "I can do that. I have to do some things in town, and I can work my schedule around to meet up then. I'll have Gibb with me if that's all right."

"Yes, ma'am, that's fine and dandy. I know that I'd feel better if he was with you. But like I said, he's going to be behind bars and won't be able to get to you." He laughed again. "I don't think that Mr. Farley will be all that happy that you'll be bringing in that husband of yours, but I wouldn't care if I was you. He's going away, and after today, it won't matter a hill of beans what he wants anymore."

"All right. I'll see you then." She turned and looked at the kids as Gibb was driving them to the school. "I'm going to go and tell off your uncle today. Anything you want me to say to him while I'm there?"

"Tell him that we all want to thank him." She asked Thad what he meant by that. "Without him being a mean person, we'd never have met Dad here. You'd not be smiling all the time, and we'd still be living in that tiny house. You tell him that we all thank him for making our lives what it was on account of us being happier than—" He looked at his sisters.

"A bug in a run in front of a fire. Why can't you remember that one?" Belle looked at her. "We hear things like that all the time from the uncles. They said that they got it from their upbringing. I write them down, so I know who told me. Thad says he'll remember. Like that is working." They were laughing as they pulled up in front of the school. "See you guys later. Mom, just spend the money. It'll be all right."

When the two of them were alone in the car, she turned to look at Gibb. It surprised her every time she looked at him that he belonged to her. That's what he told her, too. That he belonged to her. When he asked if he had egg on his face, she shook her head and decided that it was high time she had a talk with him.

"I was never married to Burney Archer, the kids' dad. Dave introduced us, and I didn't want to go out with him a second time. Then one night, he came into my apartment and raped me. Telling me the entire time that he was the one who would decide who I'd see or not. Now that he's back in prison, I sleep better, but he is due to get out soon. I didn't tell the kids that. They think that he's in for life." Gibb asked her if he had been the one who had beaten her up previously. "Yes. He and my brother. I did put his name on their birth certificates. On the off chance that I'd get some support from him. But it never came after the first couple of months. I think that Dave had something to do with that, too."

"More than likely." She watched the streets as they drove out of Gatlinburg. The snow was just starting to come down when he pulled into a car dealership parking lot outside of town. "I'm only going to suggest this to you, but I want you to be extra careful when you're out. Alone or with the kids. Burney was released just yesterday. I asked Jamie about it, and she found it just now for me. Also, I want you to consider working for the shop. You don't have to, but it would be wonderful if we had family working there. Also, you'd have free reign of it. Do what you want and order what you need. Mark said that he'd talk to you about pay. And we have to pay you because we need to show that as a loss. The store does great. Very well, as a matter of fact. You won't be bored. I promise you that."

After he got out of the car, he came around to her side and opened the door for her. No one, not in all her life, had anyone done that for her. When he put his hand out to help her out, she nearly kissed his hand, wanting to thank him for being such a wonderful person to her. It hit her then that she had fallen in love with the man.

Maddy didn't know how that had happened. She'd only been around him for a couple of weeks. But as it was right now, she didn't think that she could ever remember a time when she needed someone in her life as much as she did this man. As they looked at cars for her, all she could focus on was that she was in love for the first time in her life. And she couldn't have been happier with who she was in love with either.

"Are you all right?" She smiled up at Gibb. "You have a look on your face that I've never seen before. Should I be worried?"

"No. It's a look that I've never had before either." He smiled bigger at her. "I've fallen in love with you, Gibb Cross. I don't know how or even when, but I've never loved nor will I ever love someone as much as I do you right now."

He picked her up. After swinging her around,

laughter all around her, he put her on the ground and kissed her. It wasn't a needy kiss, nor one that he'd given her before, like a peck on her nose or mouth, but one of being in love with her, too.

"I do love you, Maddy. I have since the first time I saw you." He laughed hard like he'd only just discovered that he could. "I love Maddy Cross," he shouted. And she'd never been happier.

Chapter 4

Dave didn't care for the way that he was being treated. First of all, he was sick of bologna sandwiches. The chips were all right. Sometimes, he'd have sour cream and onion, but there were the BBQ ones that he dearly loved. It was the meat and the bread that was making him pissed off. No mayo or mustard on the sandwich, just in those hard-to-open little packets. Instead of being easy to open, he usually wore about half of it down his front when opening them. Also, the fact that he could only have bottled water—no pops or beers—made eating them all the more boring.

"Hey. You there. What's a man gotta do to get better food around here?" The guard, as usual, didn't speak. "I'm talking to you, you bastard. The least you can do is acknowledge me. My taxes pay your wages. I know that for a fact."

"Since you've never filed your taxes, from what I've heard, then no, you don't pay his wages. What is it you want, Dave? I'm having a good day, and spending any part of it with you is taking away from my happiness just being in the same general area as you are." He eyed the woman standing there. "I'm Maddy, you fucking idiot. If you can't recognize me, why the hell did you tell them that you wanted to talk to me? As I said, I'm busy."

"You sure have gotten mouthy, haven't you? I guess I'll have to beat that out of you when I get out of here. Again." He noticed that a man was hanging around by her. "You go on back to your job, bozo. I'm talking to my sister right now. Go away. We have business to discuss. I won't have you interrupting us when I tell her what she's going to be doing for me."

"Good luck with telling her what to do. And she's my wife, so no, I'm not going anywhere until you've told her or asked her, so be done with it so we can go out to lunch." He didn't know why he asked, but he wanted to know where they were going and what they were going to have. "I don't know. There is a seafood place not far from here. The two of us might end up there. Maddy, they have the best crab cakes I've ever eaten. How about that for lunch?"

"Oh yes. I've not had a good crab sandwich in a long time. You might not know this, but the kids all love seafood." He told her that he'd keep that in mind. "Right. Friday night. The kids will be so—"

"Shut the fuck up, the two of you. Christ. Who the fuck cares what your brats want? I don't. But speaking of them, I want you to have them find me a bit of cash. Well, a lot of it, actually. I have a few palms to grease to get myself out of here." She asked him what he was talking about. "Them damned brats of yours. They know what to do. And so you know, don't get all cozy with them being around either. I'm going to make it so that you're accused of being unfit so that they'll come to me. See that they don't. You're about as dumb as a post for not getting as much out of them as you can. I'm not going to waste their God-given talent like you've been doing. Does this so-called husband of yours know what they can do? I bet you kept that little bit to yourself, didn't you? Maddy don't want her little ones to be abused. Dumb ass."

"He knows and has already told them that he doesn't need them to play tricks for him. Also, they won't come to you at all now, Dave. I have a husband that they love as much as they do me. Besides, I don't know how you think that you'd be any less unfit than you're claiming that I am. I'm not the one up on forty murder charges currently sitting in a jail cell, ready to be transported to a federal prison. Not to mention all the other things that they have against you." He said that was why he wanted her to use the kids to get him some money. "Are you actually telling me to use my children to get you money so that you can get out of jail and take them from me? Is that your plan, Dave?"

"Of course it is. Isn't that what I've been telling you all along? You no more deserve those brats than you do trying to make Barney pay you child support. He's not going to do it just so you know. And I know where you live now, Maddy, so when he gets out, he's going to come gunning for you. I plan on being there, too, when he comes around. You know that he doesn't care for you making trouble for either of us. He'll make you pay." She asked him where she lived if he knew so much. "On some mountain top with a bunch of hillbillies."

He eyed the man who was with his sister. Dave knew quality clothing when he saw it, and this man *and* his sister were wearing top of the line. What the other officers were saying about the Cross people might be true. They might have more money than they needed. They'd not said that exactly, but he knew it to be a fact. He looked at Maddy while she and that man were talking again about lunch again. What the fuck was a crab sandwich anyway?

There was something different about Maddy he was only just noticing. He couldn't quite put his finger on it, but he knew that she'd had some work done on her or something. She was…well, he didn't know that what he was thinking was right or not, but she looked brighter. Like the sun only shown on her. Knowing that sounded hokey, he shook that notion out of his head. He asked her what she was going to do to help him get out of there.

"Nothing. I love that you're not roaming the streets causing any trouble." He told her that she wasn't being right. "Right or not, Dave, I'm glad that I don't have to be constantly looking over my shoulder to see where you are. Knowing that you're in here, our kids sleep better, too. They're also doing very well since you didn't ask. Sleeping better. Eating well. It's amazing what having trust in someone can do for your total well-being."

"That's what somebody said to me before. Like I had anything to do with them having sleepless nights. I made sure they were fed and watered when they were with me." She asked him if he really did put a bowl of water and food out for them on a sheet of newspaper. "Yes. They don't need to have a fancy meal all the time. Besides, I had to make sure they knew who was in charge, didn't I? If you turn them over to me, Maddy, I'll make sure that I murder you fast. I mean, I'll murder you fast." He started cursing. "Damn, woman. I can't lie, no matter who I'm talking to. I'm going to find her, too, and make her take this shit away from me. I can't do any kind of business with me having to tell the truth all the time."

"I kind of like it now that you mention it." She sat down in a chair that he knew hadn't been there before. "In fact, I have a few questions of my own to ask you. Did you kill Mom and Dad?"

"Yes." He eyed the guard standing there and then remembered he'd answered that question a few days ago with the Feds. It wasn't like they could charge him twice for admitting that he'd murdered them. "They were holding me back in getting things done the way that I wanted them. Did you know that Grandpa and Grandma left you a bunch of money? They wouldn't let me have it. So I killed Mom and Dad when they wouldn't tell me where it was. Well, that's actually how I found out about you getting it all. Hell, I didn't even know the idiot old buzzards had two cents between them. They were sure stingy about money, that's for sure. Mom and Dad were a waste of space anyway. Always harping on me to get a good job and stop robbing people. I sure showed them what sort of job I was fit for, didn't I?"

"Did you kill them, too, grandpa and grandma?" He said he'd only killed Grandpa. He'd caught him in the middle of killing the mailman. "What reason did you have to kill the mailman? He more than likely didn't know who you were from anyone else."

"You'd be wrong about that. Everyone knew who I was and what I wanted. They knew better than to cross me." He thought of how the people of their town would run and hide when he came into town. "They knew how to respect someone of higher intelligence than them. They worshiped me. At least, that's what I keep telling myself. They were afraid of me, and I damn well deserved it too. Christ, when I think of being able to get a seat at any restaurant I wanted, no matter how busy it was. You've no idea how much I loved that kind of service. I'd still have it, too, if not for you making things difficult for me."

"You must really think that, or you couldn't say it." He didn't understand what the man meant by that but let it go. "Tell me something, Dave. When the kids were with you, did you ever think that they might miss their mom? That they might need a hug from you?"

"Hell no. I didn't care that they missed their mom. I didn't understand it, so I didn't care. As for hugging them? Well, that's another hell no. I would rather have a snake curled up beside me than a kid's dirty hands touching me. Kids are nothing but germ factories, and you know that too." He laughed a little. "I'm guessing that you live for their hugs. That you even kiss them goodnight when you put them to bed. Just like I thought you were. You're a sap."

"I do, actually. And since I've adopted them, they call me Dad. Best feeling in the world if you ask me." He told him that nobody had. "All the same, I love them. And will love them forever, too."

"Like I said, you're a sap." Standing up, the guard did his usual thing. Turned with his gun pointed right at his head. "I can't get to her. Just slow your roll, why don't you? Christ, you'd think that I was armed and dangerous."

Of course, he continued to hold his gun

pointed at him. It wasn't until he sat back down that the moron finally turned his back on him and put his gun back at his chest. Shaking his head, he pointed out that he was no more dangerous to his sister than he was. At least while he was locked up.

"Yes, because that will make him feel better." He told Maddy to shut up. "Thank you. I think I will. The next time you get it into your head to call for me to tell me you want my children, forget it. I'm not coming back."

"What about the money?" She asked him what money. "Damn it, Maddy. The money that you're going to have the kids get me. That money. It's a wonder that you even know how to feed yourself. You're as dumb as a post. Get them to use their whatever it is they used that one time I had them and get me money. I'm going to need a lot of it, too. It's not as cheap as it was, paying off the dimwits in my town. These men are expensive."

"I'm thinking that you couldn't get enough money to pay them off. Or grease their palms, as you've been saying." Dave told the other man that he'd not asked him. "No, but you're referring to a federal officer to which I'm one. We swore to uphold the law against people like you."

"Well, la-de-da for you. They have their price. Just like you will when I come for the kids. You be thinking on it real hard on what you want." Dave just then thought of something. "Hey, we're related, you and me. You should do it for me for that reason alone. Since we're family and all."

"You're nothing to me. Nor are you to my kids." He asked if his kids had any special talents. "In that they love their mother and I, no, they're just normal kids."

"You're talking about Maddy's kids then. They're not yours, dumb ass. They're hers and Barney's." It hit him like it had been staring him in the face all this time. "And I just had me an epiphany. He's their daddy. I can just have him sign them over to me. It won't cost me as much as I'm betting you'll want. Christ, I don't know why I didn't think of that before."

He was still talking about how Barney would help him out with this for a few bucks when he noticed that his sister and that man were gone. Asking the guard when they'd left was a waste of time, so he didn't bother. But this Barney thing? Well, that was worth thinking about. He'd just have to get a message to him as soon as he could. Christ, oh mighty, this was working out much better than he could have hoped.

His lunch came and went. Dave didn't want to bother with another sandwich, so he left it on the tray. By this time tomorrow, he'd have all the money in the world. Yes, sir-e-Bob, he'd be rolling in the dough. The first thing he was going to do after having the kids do what he wanted he was going to treat himself to a porterhouse steak. The fattest baked potato that was ever grown, as well as slices of fried bacon that he could chop up all over it. Mushrooms too. He did love him a good mushroom sauce over his steak. His mouth was watering just thinking about it.

The rest of the afternoon into the evening, he barely paid attention to what was going on around him. There was a guard change that he missed, as well as dinner coming. Picking at it, disappointed that it wasn't the steak that he'd been drooling about all day, he ended up eating the French fries and part of the burger. They'd not given him any cheese on it or no catsup either. Sorry excuse for a dinner if he ever seen one.

Tomorrow, he kept telling himself. Tomorrow, he'd be sitting pretty. And he'd have the brats, too. Christ, he wished that he'd thought of Barney before now. It would have saved him a lot of heartache chasing after Maddy all the time, that was for sure.

~*~

Thad watched Mr. David chopping wood. He didn't know this man very well. Hardly at all, but he watched him every day doing the chopping. When he'd asked his sisters about him, Belle told him that he had some things to work out. That he was a man that had a broken heart. Today, Thad decided he was going to have to talk to the man. Time was running out for things.

When he laid down the ax and sat down on the stump that was close to him, Thad waited to see if he was going to pick it up again. It had been the third time that he'd done that, and he quickly picked up the ax and began chopping again. When he didn't this time, he made himself known to the man and walked to where he was sitting.

"Hello there, young man. You must be Gibb's little boy. My name is David. I've heard that you're fitting in all right around here with your two sisters." He said that they were and that he was glad that Dad had found them. "He's a good man. I'm sure you know that by now. What can I do for you?"

"Do you know about me and my sisters?"

He said only in that they were Gibb and Maddy's children. "Nobody told you anything else about us? How we can see things sometimes?"

It was important to know whether or not the man believed him or not before he spoke to him. When he asked what he was talking about, Thad was both relieved and worried at the same time. Relieved because he didn't say that he didn't believe what he'd heard and worried because he might not believe what he had to tell him. Instead of leaving, like he was ready to do, he nodded and began with his tale to the other man.

"My sisters and I are triplets. I guess you might know that, but what you don't know, and even our mom doesn't know, is that we could talk to each other before we were born. We could talk to Mom, too, but it was only to let her know not to do something that would be a danger to her or us." The man nodded, saying nothing yet. "We knew that we were special before we were born. Even in the hospital, we told the nurses which baby was sick and which needed extra care. Diaper changes and little stuff like that. They did a good job there. Even when someone came to see the babies that shouldn't have been there, we told them about it. Mr. David, we've never told anyone this before."

"I see. And I'm guessing that you have a reason for telling me now." Thad nodded. "Is this dangerous, whatever you're going to tell me?"

"Yes, sir. Not for you but for this woman that is living in town. You have to go and help her. If you don't, it'll be all right if you say no. But I guess, but she'll die. My sisters and I, we've been trying to take care of her since we've been here. Now we can't do it anymore without you helping us."

David stood up. So did Thad. Turning to go to the house, wondering if he'd been an adult if someone would believe him then, his heart hurt for the—

"Aren't we going to save her?" Thad turned to look at David. "You said that she needed my help. I'm assuming that it needs to happen today, or you wouldn't have come out here three times to tell me. Why didn't you just say my name, Thad? I would have stopped to talk to you."

"I don't know you." David said that was his fault, that he'd been working through some stuff. "Yeah. My sister, Maria, she said to tell you that your wife wasn't happy for a long time."

David sat down again, narrowly missing the ax

this time. Thad went to him, making sure that he was all right. When David asked him how he'd known about his wife, he sat back down on the log to tell him what he knew.

"Her name was Lily. Right?" David nodded. "Yeah, we thought that was your wife. Maria, she could talk to her a lot. She has this sort of radar thing that reaches out to people before they die like your wife did. Sometimes, she can talk them out of it, but Ms. Lily she was too sad for her to be able to talk her into not doing that. Her heart was broken, Maria said."

"Your sister tried to talk her out of killing herself?" Thad said that they could all do it and did. But Maria was stronger at it. "What did she say to her? Did...did Lily say why she didn't talk to me first?"

"She said that her heart was broken because you were so sad." David was crying now, and it hurt Thad that he was the cause of the man's pain. "Don't cry, Mr. David. I'm only telling you this because Maria said that you'd need to know it. It's not a bad thing to have spoken to her for you, right?"

"No. It's all right. Tell me what she said to Maria, please? You said that her heart was broken for me. Did she say why?" He nodded, and Mr. David sobbed loudly. Then he pulled him off the stump and held him to him tightly. "Tell me, please? Even if you think it will hurt me."

"She said that her heart was broken because she had been such a burden to you. Maria, she told her that you'd not think that. That you loved her to pieces, but she told her that it was costing the two of you too much for her to be sick like this. Not money, she told my sister, but of life. That the pain of watching you see her suffer was hurting her deep in her soul. Lily said that the only way that she could be happy in Heaven was to set you free." He let Mr. David cry.

It hurt him to hear an adult cry like he was. Great sobs that even made him want to cry with him. When Dad joined them there, Mr. David grabbed onto him and held him while he told him what he'd said.

"She did this for me. I knew that she had in some way, but to know that...she set me free, Gibb. So that I'd not hurt anymore. And it's all I have been doing is hurting because I've let her down."

"No, you didn't." Thad watched as Maria smiled at David. "She told me that you'd say that.

That you let her down. She wanted me to tell you that she loved you dearly, Mr. David, but she wasn't in love with you. I don't know what that means, but she said to tell you that and that you'd agree with her. Ms. Lily said that you loved her, too, but you weren't in love with her anymore. That your heart was too burdened to be in love with anyone. She didn't want that for you either. That's why she set you free."

"But I did love her." Maria looked at Thad, then back at David. He stared at them both before he nodded. "No. I think you're right. I never...I did love her. More than anything. But I wasn't in love with her anymore. She was...she wasn't my heart anymore but the person that I loved because I had for so long."

Neither of them said anything. Thad was glad that Maria came out to help him, but he really needed Mr. David to help the lady in town. He seemed to understand that about the time that Belle joined them. Wiping his eyes, he asked where they were going to go.

"Her name is Rusty." He told him that he didn't know her last name but gave him the address. Dad loaded them up in the car, and they were all five headed out when he remembered that he'd not told his mom where they were going. Dad said that he'd make sure that she knew, and they were all right with that. Thad wondered if he should have told him the rest of the story of Rusty. But Belle told him that they'd figure it out soon enough. He hoped so. Thad had never seen a little baby before.

As soon as they pulled up in front of the house, he knew that they were going to make it for Rusty. While he knew absolutely nothing about babies, he did know that Mr. David did. Belle told him that he'd almost been a doctor and that he'd delivered three babies when he'd been practicing. Asking his sister how long ago that had been, she patted him on the arm and said not much had changed. Like she would know, he thought. But wisely kept his mouth shut.

"We have to hurry." Even as they were going in the front of the abandoned house, Thad could feel her pain. It took his breath away when they went inside, and he found himself pushing Dad and Mr. David up in front of him. Hurry, his mind kept yelling at him. Hurry. Hurry.

When Ms. Rusty screamed, Dad looked at him, and he told him to hurry. As soon as they busted the bedroom door open, Ms. Rusty was soaking wet with sweat and pain. Dad looked at him.

"Did you know this part?" He nodded. "Then why didn't you have us call an ambulance. It would have been better for her." Thad started to tell him that it wouldn't have been for the baby when Belle told Mr. David to help her. "David, do you know how to deliver a baby?"

"I do. I honestly do. My goodness, this is what I was needed for." The two of them set to work. Maria called for Aunt Amelia, and she was able to give them all the things that they'd need to deliver the little boy. As soon as he started crying, everyone in the room, except for Rusty, started laughing. She was lying on the dirty floor, sleeping.

While they were all looking over the little boy, he and his sisters explained why they'd not been able to call an ambulance. Rusty was fine with having her son, but the people that she was having it for weren't all that thrilled.

"She was a surrogate for them." Thad looked at Belle when he told them that part. Nodding with her, he continued. "I don't know their names, but Rusty, her last name is Crawford, was going to be paid for having this little boy. Then the people got a divorce, and the missus told her to get rid of him. She wouldn't do that on account of her being his momma. Anyway, she's been hiding out so that he'd be safe. Her daddy knows that she's been hiding out, but he's sick too and needs her to come home. Ms. Rusty is terrified that the people will hurt them. But she's more worried about the baby."

"That's not a great deal of information, is it, son?" Dad laughed when he looked at Mr. David. "I'd say that we should get this little one and his momma home and then figure out where to find her father. I'm assuming, though, I don't know why, but it's important to this family to make sure that they're all three healthy and happy."

"I don't know that part either." Belle looked at Maria before she spoke again. "Dad, Ms. Rusty can't go to the hospital. They have some man looking at the records for hospitals to find her. I know this man is magical, but nothing much else. We've been keeping an eye on Ms. Rusty for a few weeks now. Just making sure that she's warm and stuff. I sure am glad to know that she's going to be staying with us now. She'll be just fine."

Uncle Frazier showed up a few minutes after the little boy was wrapped up and taken home. Once Ms. Rusty disappeared, too, Dad and Mr. David cleaned up the room so that it wouldn't be considered a crime scene if anyone came up here looking around. After that was finished up, they went back to the mountain top.

Thad loved this family. More than he ever thought that he would when they were getting hints about their dad and his brothers. They weren't just good people, but they were good to everyone and everything. Even the land and animals that lived around them. The Cross family, too, cared that they were taken care of as well. Sitting in the chair, taking his turn to watch over Ms. Rusty, he did wonder a little if she was going to be his aunt, too. He'd have to talk to Maria about it. She usually had that sort of information before he or Belle did.

Chapter 5

Gibb had been asked to come into the forestry office today. He'd given his notice some time ago and had worked it out. But today, first thing after entering the greenhouse, he'd been asked to come to the office. He didn't know what it was, but he did have assurances from Belle that things were just fine.

He'd come to depend on his little family for a lot of things. Not once had he asked them for information. It felt like he was pushing boundaries that he didn't think he should if he'd done that. But they would come to him a couple of times a week and tell him this or that. Like general information that they thought that he should know. Like after breakfast today.

"Dad, when you get a call from someone by the name of Agent Blackstone, don't freak out." He said that he was the retired regional manager for this area of the forest department. "Yeah, that's who I think he is. He isn't going to hurt you or anything. There are just a few questions that he has. I don't know what about, but it'll be all right."

The other day, it had been Maria who had told her mom that she needed to go to the shop today. That there was someone there that needed her help. Turned out to be just fine, just as she said it would, and they had a new vendor for tea. A mountain man had asked if he could put his flower teas in the store to sell. Gibb had been happy about that. It meant that they could take what little hadn't sold of Granny's tea home with them and treasure it.

It was Belle, too, who said she knew what was needed to continue making the tea that everyone liked, which herb or flower, as well as how much was put in. Gibb couldn't have been happier if she'd told him that she knew the secret to the meaning of life. He'd not asked her if she did actually know the meaning. Frankly, he was slightly afraid that they might well know the answer.

"Agent Cross? My name is Agent Blackstone." He shook the man's hand and felt a little bit of something that didn't seem right. He wasn't nervous, but he wasn't sure what he was supposed to do with the feeling. "I've come here on a special mission from my boss. He wants me to talk to you about heading up a Search and Rescue team for the mountains. Not just your mountain but all the national parks. I know that we have quite a few people who go missing yearly, from all of them annually that usually turn up. However, he wants this to be something that he can call on for everywhere someone might have taken a wrong turn and ended up someplace they might not know how to get back from. He wanted to see if, with you and your families' help, we could lower that number."

"I'm not sure what I can do to head that sort of group up. I do know that all the parks have their own teams. And that the federal officers who work there have been trained on how to do a search for people missing. As you said, they usually turn up on their own." He nodded and told him that although it would be a mountain team, they'd be used for all kinds of terrain and weather. "All right. I can help you out with that. As you know, my brothers and I have retired from the park service. We can guide you in the right direction in finding people that will do this for you, but—"

"Dad, he's looking for someone specific." He asked

Belle who and asked Agent Blackstone if he'd like to get some lunch so that he could buy himself time to talk to Belle. *"He's thinking that Ms. Rusty is hiding in the park. He wants you and the others to come out of retirement to find her for him. It's his daughter that hired Ms. Rusty to have her baby for her. He doesn't know the facts of what they want with the baby, but he is willing to do this for her. He's dying. Hoping to see his grandson before he dies."*

"Honey, what should I do here? I'm not going to give him anything in the event it gets back to his daughter. While I know there are two sides to every story, Rusty strikes me as the injured party here in that she was willing to have a baby by herself in an abandoned building. Someone has to be powerfully scared to do that." Belle said that he was right. Not to trust him. He was a liar already. *"He might not be a liar all the time, but someone that believes his child. "No. He's a liar. He lied to a lot of people just to get your name. I'm sorry, Dad. I hadn't any idea when I told you you'd be all right."*

"I'm having lunch with him now." They were seated right away because of who he'd been around here. As soon as he was seated with the man, he asked if he needed his brothers. *"I mean, I don't think he'll hurt me in public, but I just don't know about people*

anymore."

"*I don't know them at all. Mom and the Aunts are in town. I'm sending them to you. They'll take care of him.*" That scared him more than the thought of him getting hurt. The women were very protective of them, even though they were all large black bears. Belle laughed. "*They'll be all right. They won't hurt him too much.*"

Before he could ask her what she meant by that, the women showed up in force. The four of them were the most beautiful women he'd ever seen, but they were also the scariest group he'd ever encountered too.

"Hello there." He kissed his wife and hugged the other women. Before he could introduce the women to Blackstone, it was Maddy who sat down at the table first, with the others following. Smiling at him, she turned to Blackstone. "You're an idiot if you think that your daughter is a sweet little thing that you want to believe that she is. You've enough clues throughout her life that you know just what sort of person she is. Also, her soon to be ex-husband is a nice guy that is being given a bad rep because you've got your head so far up your ass about little Paige that you can't see what he is really like."

"What are you talking about? I'm here to talk to this man, and I don't remember inviting you. Besides, I don't know what you think you're telling me about my little girl, but she's a good girl. That husband of hers knocked her around, and she's finally seeing the light and leaving him." It was Amelia who shook her head and then touched her fingers to Blackstone's. He sat there quietly for long enough for the women to order with him and order for Blackstone as well. When he finally came out of what appeared to be a trance, he sat there for so long that Gibb was worried for the man.

"Where did you...what did you do to me?" Amelia told him that she only reminded him what he already knew. "I remember that day. Paige said that Howard started it."

"Did it look like he started anything with her? Not to mention, you know too that Paige can have as many children as she wants. She just didn't want to have to give up her fun in order to carry it to term. She's also planning to kill the little boy if he's given to her. Because she's not a good person." Blackstone sat there for several more minutes. He was a thinker, Gibb surmised and was glad that he wasn't just spouting off things to piss everyone off. "Also,

Danny, you might want to remember that incident that happened two weeks ago. You know as well as I do that your cook just didn't fall. Paige hurt her as she has many times over the years. And her fun is dangerous, too. She's been hurting the children of your town for decades."

"I didn't know." It was Maddy who slapped the man. She'd been the closest, or one of the others might have. "All right. You've made your point. But I'm a dying old man, and I won't get to see him."

"What is more important to you, Danny? The safety of your grandson or you seeing him? And you're not dying anymore. You were, but I fixed it so that you can live just a few months more. I have the ability to give you a lifetime with Joey, but I will take what I've given you and more if you even think of answering that call from your daughter." Just then, a cell phone started twittering. "You can answer it. But do not mention anything that I've told you. And yes, his name is Joey."

While Blackstone spoke to who Gibb assumed was his daughter, he talked to the women. Not about the man or his grandchild but about the upcoming dinner they were all having together. It was going to be a life celebration for his grandparents. Yesterday,

Mark had remembered that tomorrow was Granny and Grandda's anniversary. They wanted to celebrate it as a family. When Danny put his cell phone on the table, he looked at all of them.

"I don't know what to do." Jamie told him that he did know what to do. He just needed to get his balls out of his pocket and do it. "You four are very outspoken, aren't you? I mean, I've been verbally abused, physically too and threatened. Did I miss anything?"

"Yes, two very important things that you should forever remember. You've got a grandson, and if you play this right, you might get to see him if I don't put you in an early grave." Gibb couldn't help it. He didn't know if it was the expression on Danny's face or just the general conversation that he was having with his sisters, but he burst out laughing. "That is my husband telling you that you have to find the humor in things, or you really will end up dead. Danny, when was the last time you had a good time with your daughter? Or, for that matter, have you ever reached out to your son-in-law and spoken to him about the actions of what your daughter is telling you? From what I've gathered, he's a good man and had honestly loved Paige. That is until she started showing him her true colors. He'd be a good man to have in your corner."

"I did like him." No one said anything as their meals were brought to him. Danny was nearly finished with his meal of a burger and fries when he turned to Amelia. "What do you mean, I'm not dying anymore? The doctor just told me today that I only have weeks to live."

"You have months now. No more than that if you don't do something about Paige." He reminded her that she was still his daughter. "Yes. She is. There is no disputing that. However, she's seriously not a good person. In fact, she's a murderer. And I believe that you're well aware of it."

They finished their meals. Danny didn't contribute much, hardly anything at all, actually. But once they were cleared of their plates and talking about the dinner, he seemed to wake up. Looking at him, he told him the real reason that he'd wanted him to set up the rescue team, as well as the fact that his daughter had wanted her son.

"Yes, she does, but not to raise. I believe you know that now." He nodded and looked so sad that Gibb found himself wanting to hug him, telling him that it would be all right. "What are you going to do,

Danny? I want you to know that once we leave here, if you decide to pursue this, you'll never see him or the woman who gave birth to him."

"Rusty Crawford. I liked her. Even after doing an extensive background check on her, I still liked her. Not only did I find out why she'd risk so much in doing this for Paige, but she also has a good heart. My thinking now is that she hadn't any idea what Paige would have done. Or she wouldn't have done it. She's desperate to pay off her loans, but she's far from stupid. Rusty is doing this for the sole reason of paying off her student loans. I suppose you know where she is, too." No one said a word. "You know, I don't know that I would tell me either. I won't help Paige, but I guess it would still take more than my word to convince you of that. I would love to see him, Joey, I mean. I also know that's not going to happen either. But if Rusty or Joey need anything, you tell me, and I'll get it to them."

Jamie handed him her cell phone. Danny just stared at what he was sure was a picture of Joey for the longest time before he started to sob. Telling them that he looked so much like Howard that he could have been his twin made them all laugh a little.

After he handed back her phone, Danny said

that he was going to take care of things right now. He also gave them the phone number and address of Howard. Telling them again that he was a good man who had been duped. After Danny left them, telling him that he'd be in touch, the other women left him, and it was just him and Maddy.

"I want to have a baby with you. Soon. Like, I'm thinking that we can start on that today if you're not too busy." He signaled for the check, which made her laugh. "I love you so much, Gibb Cross. I love too that you're so good to me and the kids."

"I love you. And I love them. But if we don't get home soon, we're never going to be allowed in this place again. I'm going to toss you to the floor and take you right here in front of everyone." She stood up and smiled. Once he had the check paid, leaving a larger than normal tip to the staff, they were headed out the door. His cell phone ringing when he got in his car had him whimper.

"Can we stay all night at Uncle Frazier's house tonight? He said that he'd even take us to school in the morning so you don't have to come and get us." He asked Thad if he'd spoken to his mom. "Yeah, she was weird about it too. She said to ask you, and you'd better say yes. Why didn't she just say yes?

I've said this before, I think, but women are weird."

"Yes. You can spend the night. But you make sure that your uncle knows that if something comes up, he can call, and I'll take you guys." He said that he'd tell them. They were going to work in his studio tonight. "That reminds me. We have the builders coming out this weekend to have the building put up for you guys and your mom. She wants to put an office out in it so that she can have a separate place for working. All right."

After hanging up with Thad, Gibb found himself whistling all the way home. He'd been waiting for this day for what seemed like years, and he was going to be good at it. Stopping by a couple of the specialty shops, he picked up some champagne, chocolate and even a tray already made up of cheese and crackers. It wouldn't be his family's brands, but it would hold them throughout the night. He hoped so anyway.

~*~

Maddy didn't have any idea what was sexy anymore. She was the mother of ten-year-old triplets and hadn't been on a date…well, she'd never been on a real date since before they'd been born. A couple of work meet-ups. A function that she'd ask a co-worker to, and that was about it. She didn't count blind dates. They usually had the man thinking that it was him paying for dinner and her being so grateful that she'd fall right into bed with him. Nope.

Gibb wouldn't care, she supposed, about what she wore to bed. She'd been putting the man off for a while and figured that he'd just wam-bam, thank you, ma'am, and that would be all for some reason that had her giggling. Gibb didn't strike her as rushing through anything once he set his mind to it.

Finally giving up on how to pose herself, she stripped down, popped into a quick shower and wrapped a towel around her. It was, she figured, about as sexy as she could look without having a nighty or something like that.

She was still in the bathroom, blowing dry her hair, when she heard Gibb come into the room. He was either talking to her or himself, so she had to turn the dryer off to hear him. Stepping into the bedroom with him, Maddy watched what he was doing for several minutes while he fussed around the room.

He had a bouquet of flowers in his hand, trying his best to stuff them into a too-small vase. Under his arm was the largest box of chocolates that she'd ever seen. She thought she saw that it weighed eight pounds but figured that had to be wrong. Eight pounds of chocolate? Then there was the 'thank you' bag filled with who knew what that was lying on the bed. Going there, she dumped it out to see what it was.

"I got us some cheese and crackers. But on the way home, I tried one of the crackers and had to spit it out. I think I've figured out all on my own why the homemade crackers that we sell are such a hit. Those are, simply put, nasty. And don't get me started on the cheese." He came to her, digging something out of his pocket. "Here. Let me cut you a piece, and you tell me what you think? If I'm right, I'm going to have you double the amount of crackers at the shop while putting some of these next to them. People will be buying them in bulk."

The cheese wasn't that bad. But then, she'd not had any of the stuff they made here on the mountain. The crackers were bad. They were stale, first of all, and flavorless. Putting the entire purchase back in the bag, she dumped it into the trash. Then she took a good look at the chocolates.

"This says there are eight pounds in here, Gibb. Do you even like chocolate enough to eat eight pounds of it?" He said he got it for her. "I *can't* eat eight pounds of that either. I'd be as big as a motel."

"Oh, no. You'll not gain any weight now that we're mates. I don't know if it has anything to do with us burning up more energy or something like that, but you won't gain any weight until you have a baby. And that goes away really fast. Or so I found out." She asked him who he'd asked. "Mark. But he'd asked Granny and Grandda. We don't have a lot of information about raising cubs because our parents weren't around. Also, the only contact that I've had with cubs are usually in the park. However, they're just cubs and not shifters. You look good enough to eat right now. You've not changed your mind, have you?"

"No. I was debating on how to look sexy for you. I don't know that I pulled it off with just a towel. What do you think?" He asked her to model her towel for him by turning around full circle. "Well? Too much? Not enough? I was thinking how I haven't tried to look good for a man in a very long time."

"You'd look sexy to me if you were wearing sweats and a tee shirt. I think you are absolutely the most beautiful woman in the world. No matter how you're dressed." She felt her heart melt a little with that. "It's not your body that I want. Well, that's not true. I do want to make love to you. But not because I'm this horney teenager but because I love you and want to show you how much by worshipping every inch of you. Even if I never entered you, came deep inside of you, your pleasure is all that I care about. You're my very next breath. The beating of my heart. You're also the most important person to me and will be forever. I love you, Maddy. With all that I am."

"I love you too, Gibb. And that was by and far the most sweetest declaration of love that I've ever heard or read." She moved toward him, dropping the towel as she moved. "I want us to make love. To become whole."

Gibb picked her up. Holding her high enough in front of him so that he could kiss her. As he moved her more upward, he tasted more of her. Her breasts, her skin beneath. Holding onto him as best she could, Maddy tangled her fingers into his hair and massaged his head, all the while wanting more from him. To do more to him. When he sat her down on her feet, she looked up at him and saw, just for a few seconds, his bear.

"I can see him." Gibb nodded as he continued to stare at her. "Someday, I'd like to see him, touch him. If that would be all right?"

"Yes." This time, when he picked her up, he gently laid her down on their bed. It was bigger than any bed that she'd seen before, and she knew that they'd give the mattress a good workout before morning. Sitting up on her elbows behind her, Maddy watched as he pulled one button at a time from his shirt and striped it off. Then his belt.

She wasn't going to make it, she decided, when he pulled his belt from the loops of his pants. Slowly, like he was weaving a magical spell for her to be enchanted by. The way that she was feeling in that moment, Maddy could have come and come hard just by looking at him.

Gibb had the body of a god. His muscles were well defined, and his arms were strong, unlike a bodybuilder, but naturally and fully formed. Even his fingers that were touching her face were strong and callused. His work around the farm had made him into someone who would be both envied as well as worshipped. Gibb was an Adonis.

He got to his knees then, pulling her naked, over-warm body to the edge so that her legs dangled off from the side. As he massaged her feet, then calves, as well as her thighs, he never took his eyes off of hers. Even as he gently pulled her legs apart, exposing parts of her body that she felt wetting even more, she could have no more denied him than she wanted him to stop. Her need to have him touch her in any way possible was beyond her control. And she loved it.

The lick to her thighs couldn't have prepared her for his next move. As he slid his hand up to her apex, he licked her entrance until she cried out with the pleasure of it. Spreading her legs even more, giving him all that he wanted, Maddy fell back on the bed, her body suddenly weak with the need to scream and scream out her releases.

He nibbled at her clit, suckled it as well. Even as his fingers slid in and out of her, she rode his hand. Every time that she felt the slight tingle of release, even when her body seemed to ready itself for him, she would cry and beg him for more. And he obliged her.

For every climax that she had, he'd double his efforts to make her come all the harder. Losing count, not caring anymore if she lived or died when he finished with her, Maddy let her body roll and roll over the mountain of need and satisfaction again and again.

Her body was weak yet ready for more. Her mind was blank but for the endless pain/pleasure that it was experiencing. With each release, every small or large punch to her system, Maddy fell deeper and deeper in love with Gibb until she simply couldn't anymore.

Lifting his head up, yanking him up by his soft dark hair, no words were needed to tell him what she needed from him. Standing up, she moaned with a new need. His cock, stiff and hard from his body, seemed to be ready for her, and she wanted him.

Moving up onto the bed, she felt it move and sway under his weight. His body and his hands touched her as his mouth and tongue tasted hers. The need to hold onto him, to keep him as close as she could for fear of exploding, Maddy held his mouth to hers as she wrapped her legs tightly around his. His cock sliding into her made her lose her barely-held consciousness. The climax of all releases dropped her over the edge.

When she woke, Gibb was making love to her slowly. Saying her name, telling her how much he loved her. Looking up at him, his smile was all that she needed to know that what she'd said earlier was true. She did love this man more than anything in this world or the next. Wrapping her legs around him again, ridding his waves of taking her too, Maddy told him that she loved him.

"And I you. You're ready to breed love. We can make a child...I guess I should say that we've made a child." Her happiness knew no bounds then. It filled her from her toes to her head with only those few words. "I need to fill you again, love. Christ, I can't wait any longer.

He took her then. Like a man possessed, he fucked her hard. Holding on again, digging both her heels and nails into his body to keep him there, was all that she could think to do. His balls slapping hard against her ass, thinking of how full they felt to her. Then, Maddy screamed out a release that felt as if it were tearing her asunder, and there would be nothing she could do to stop it.

"Christ." Gibb filled her. Even as he slammed his cock deep into her harder than he'd done before, she came again and again. Holding onto his shoulders now, his body slick with blood and sweat, Maddy kissed him savagely and hungrily until she couldn't hold on any longer.

Gibb dropped atop her then. Even though he was quite heavy, she enjoyed the way he held her.

After he rolled to the side, her body still a part of his, he laid back on the pillows there and reached for and found them a blanket to pull over them.

Sleep had never been something that came to her easily. Nor did it feel so overwhelmingly needed. But almost as soon as she closed her eyes, she felt her body so relaxed that nothing else entered her mind. Other than, of course, she was in love with Gibb Cross.

Chapter 6

It took Gibb most of the morning to work the kinks out of his body. Even taking a hot shower had done nothing to the soreness of his body. While he sat at the planter table, he thought a great deal about Maddy. And the way that she looked when he left her this morning. It was that, he told himself, or he'd stay with her all day, making them both more sore than they were at this moment.

She'd moaned when he got out of the bed. He might well have stayed and figured out what the moaning was about when he had felt his body seize up in pain. Not just like a pulled muscle either but like his body had been pulled on a rack and that someone was trying to make him several feet taller than he was now. Moving — really, he limped all the way to the bathroom and was positive that if there hadn't been a towel in the room that he could use,

Kathi S. Barton

he was going to dress himself wet and get out of the room before he begged Maddy to make his pain go away.

It was closer to noon now, and he was feeling a good deal better than he was at eight when he'd shown up. Still sore, he figured that he'd shift. However, when he'd thought about shifting and getting rid of the rest of the pain, he felt his bear actually cringe away from being freed. As if he'd suffered as much as he did making love to their mate. Gibb screamed and then winced when someone patted him on the back.

"Are you all right?" He glared at David, telling him that he startled him, that was all. "I'm sorry. I thought you heard me come in. I was making enough noise to wake the dead."

"Sorry." He planted a few more seeds in the dirt before he took a good look at the man. "You look happy. What's going on today? Did you finally get it that you don't need to chop all the wood in one day?"

"Something like that. I've been talking to Rusty. She is the cutest little thing, don't you think?" He said she was just adorable. He'd not meant to sound so snappy, but it went right over David's head. "Anyway, she lets me hold Joey off and on. While there, she told me what was going on with the baby's father and mother. It's not hers."

"Rusty was the surrogate. I'm sure that it has her DNA." David shook his head and explained. "Oh. So it's just the father's sperm that was used to create him. The mother didn't donate any eggs? I don't know why, but I figured that was the way that it worked when you used someone else to have your child. That, I don't know, they both donated something."

"I'm not sure either, but Joey was created by using Rusty's egg and the father's donation. So, I guess what I'm trying to say is that it's Rusty and the dad's baby. Paige has no rights to the child at all. The only person that she'd dealt with and who signed the contract with her was the mister. She didn't tell me his name yet, but I'm sure she'll trust me soon enough with that. I didn't tell her that Paige and the man are divorced. Nor that her father came to see you."

"His name is Howard Crawford. He, too, has been looking for Rusty, I was told, but not to harm her in any way. He just wants to make sure that she is paid for what she has done for the two of them. It's a substantial amount of money, too. I guess that Rusty was going to stay with them for a few months in order to be able to breastfeed the baby for them." David asked him who had told him that. "Mark and Jamie. After getting his name from Rusty, not through her telling us, by the way, they did a background check. Howard is a good man by all accounts. And didn't have any idea what sort of person his wife was until it was too late. Jamie said that she only wanted the child so that she could get sympathy when it died as an infant. While in Rusty's care, of course, so that people would feel sorry for her. And Rusty would be in prison for however, Paige dreamed up the murdering of her son would be. The town that they live in is on the verge of running them out of town. Paige figured that the baby would have them like her again. Not that she liked them, but that way, their kids could come around again, and she could hurt them. And she has done that for a long time."

"So this Howard person is looking for Rusty to pay her for the job that she didn't do for them? Do you believe that?" Gibb told his friend that he honestly did. "Okay. But I like this girl and her son. If he's not on the up and up with her, then I'm going to have to kill him."

"Just like that?" David told him that he'd grown quite fond of Rusty in the last few days. "Fond of her? Or love her? You deserve either one, David. You know that, don't you?"

"Yes. And it's only a daughter-like fondness for her. I did...I hate to admit this, but I thought about falling in love with her. But first of all, I am old enough to be her father, so...gross. And secondly, I'm not ready for that yet. I've taken them both under my wing and want to treat her like the daughter I never had if she'll have me. But I do love that little man. Have you ever seen a baby with such a full head of hair before? It's like he's wearing a wig or something."

They both laughed, and Gibb could see that it had made David feel better. Not just being around the baby and his mother but to be able to be here, period. And even though they all teased him about chopping the wood all the time, it was going to come in handy this winter for not just their families but anyone in town who was in need of wood to heat their home as well. After David left him there, saying he was going into town for a few things, Gibb got back to work.

It was nearly dusk, coming along earlier, it

seemed than even yesterday. He cleaned up his work area and made his way to the house. Maddy had told him last night that she had some things to do at the shop today and wouldn't be home until late. Mark told him, too, earlier this morning that the shop was already showing a profit with having someone around as excited as Maddy seemed to be about their mountain.

"Dad, can I talk to you?" Gibb was just fixing some burgers to fry up when Maria came into the kitchen. Asking him if she could help, he showed her how to peel lettuce off the head so they could have plenty enough for their burgers. "Yesterday, when we were out in the woods, I saw a bunch of bugs. I don't guess they're bugs, really, but insects. Anyway, I was wondering if there are any bug insect shifters." He stopped what he was doing and turned to her.

"Why do you ask me that?" She looked at him seriously, then back at the lettuce and didn't answer. "You have a reason for asking me that, honey. What caused you to think about that after telling me that you'd been in the woods when you saw them. I'm not mad, Maria, but curious, that's all."

"I saw some of them that looked like little people." She continued to pull lettuce off the head until he had to put his hand over hers to stop. As it was now, they had enough for several hundred burgers as well as salads too. "They spoke to me, Dad. Like I could understand them and everything. They asked me about your granny and grandpa."

"You told them that she died." She nodded. "Did you also tell them that grandda had been killed?" She nodded again.

Gibb put the platter of burger meat on the counter and sat down. He had to think. While he'd heard of little people his entire life, he'd never actually seen one. Much less spoke to one, either. However, he also knew that they were good friends to his grandparents.

"Are you mad at me?" He said that he wasn't. He was just thinking. "The woman little person that spoke to me said that I had to take her spot. That I needed to be their helper if you would allow it. She knows who you are. She also knows Mom."

"Granny used to tell us about the little people of the mountains. Every winter, she would tell us how she had to put out food for them and when spring came, they would bless her with a plentiful garden and bountiful trees." Maria said that was what they told her. "Yes. All right. Granny also told us that they would only pick the bravest and the most pure heart to help them. That to help the faeries, that's what she called them, was something that very few people ever got to do."

"Thank you, Dad, for believing me." Maria climbed up on his lap then and hugged him. When she started speaking, Gibb held onto his daughter tightly, knowing now that she was even more special than he'd thought when he'd first met her. Maria had been chosen to watch over the little people like his granny had.

"When my granny was just a little girl, no older than you are now, she told me that she'd been out in the gardens when she found a small creature. It was shaped like a person but had the most beautiful wings that she'd ever seen. No one believed her. Everyone who came to hear about Granny and her little people would tease her and poke fun at her. Then, when she met Grandda, he saw them too. They were helpful to the little people together, and no one made fun of them again." Gibb asked Maria if her brother and sister could see them too. She told him that they both did. Then she got up but stood close to him. "What do you need to help them? I'll get you three whatever you need to make sure that they're taken care of."

"Dad, she wants to talk to you." Gibb sat up straighter in his chair. Looking around, Maria told him that he couldn't see her until he believed in her. "You do, don't you? Believe me when I tell you that I've spoken to the queen of all the little people."

"I do. I don't know why other than I think that I almost believed my granny when she would tell me about them. She never told anyone else, not my brothers either. She said that she needed for me to help her, and I did. I would gather winter flowers for them, and Granny would make sure that they were given to them. I don't know if then I really believed she needed them or was just trying to get me out of the house, but I gathered them for her."

"Her name is Roseland. She's right here." Maria reached into her pocket. When she pulled it free of the small opening, she put out her hand for him. Gibb didn't see anything, and it disappointed him all the way to his core. "Keep looking, Dad. She said that as an adult, it'll be hard for you to see her right away."

So he stared at his daughter's small hand. When he was ready to give up, thinking that he'd not had a pure enough heart, he saw a flash of something. Then more as he moved his face closer to the open palm. Then? There she was.

"My lady." He put his hand over his mouth when she put her hands over her ears. With a whisper this time, he told her that he was glad to make her acquaintance. "You're someone that I never thought to see in all my life. Welcome to our home."

"You look much like your grandda when he was a good deal younger. I am sorry for his death and that of his mate. They were more special to us and good to us than anyone has ever been before. I think you and your little ones will be even more helpful to us, too." He told her that he would do anything in his power to keep them safe. "I thank you, kind sir. If you, as you had before, are willing to find us food to eat during the winter, we will be fine. Also, some juices. We do better than well with fine juice." Gibb had a thought.

"You gave my granny the tea recipes." She bowed before him, and he laughed though quietly. "We've only a few...you also made sure that one of my children could make it, didn't you? That the tea would be there for us for a long time."

"I did. We did. It was our pleasure to do so. Your children have brought us much joy since they have been here. Just to hear their laughter, it makes our magic stronger. And the little one that is here in your house as well, he's been such a wonderful addition to our faeries."

"Is it true that only the small ones can see you without any kind of magic?" She said that infants see them the most, but yes, they can see them all. She also said that they would watch over little Joey, too, because of what he and his family had done and are currently doing for her kind. "As I said, we will do whatever you need."

"Would it be all right with you, young Gibb, if we were to live in your greenhouse in the colder months?" He said that it had heat now, and they were welcome to it. "Thank you. So very much. And in return, we will do the same for your gardens and plants that we had for your granny. But, as we did with them, you cannot tell anyone of us. Not any of your brothers. They will not understand as you have."

"What about my wife?" He heard Maddy coming through the house then. When Roseland turned when she entered the room, she bowed before Maddy. Gibb knew the exact moment that she saw the little woman. It was Maria who introduced her to the queen. Gibb, feeling good about the events, went outside to put the burgers on the grill. While he was out there, he took a look around the yard. It was then that he saw what he'd never in his life imagined himself seeing.

There were hundreds, no thousands, of the little people just beyond where he was standing. Hovering in the air about his height. The sound, he knew that he'd heard it before, was like cicadas in the summertime. A beautiful sound that made him smile. As they moved closer, almost in a swarm, he nearly dropped the platter of meat and ran for cover. But all they did was float like a smallish Christmas light in front of him. It was then that one of them landed on his hand. The door opened and closed behind him, and he knew that it was one of his children.

"Dad, don't move quickly, or you'll hurt them." Belle. He laughed a little, thinking that if he moved, they'd be all over him before he could react. However, all he did was tell his daughter that he wasn't going to harm them. "The one on your hand, her name is Strawberry. She's just getting to know what you smell like, that's all."

"I have the burgers in my hand, honey. I don't think I'll smell very good to them. Do you?" Belle laughed and told him to be careful but to cook the burgers. That she was hungry. "All right. Just, I don't know, honey, be careful that they don't want to hurt you either."

He nodded to the little creature when she flew up from his hand. Ever so gently, he put the burgers on the flame and then set the platter aside. Moving slowly, telling all that were around him what he was doing and how he was going to move, he felt silly when Strawberry landed on his shoulder. While he couldn't see her well, he knew that she was hanging onto the collar of his shirt.

"You are a good man, Lord Gibb." He said that he was just Gibb, not lord of anything. "Ah, but you are now, my lord. You have accepted us much faster than anyone has. You'll be a fine person to care for us in the coming years."

"It'll be my pleasure to help you all. I don't mind if you use the house or the greenhouse for your living space. Just, I don't know. Just not mine and my wife's bedroom. Nor the bathrooms. That's sort of a private place for us." She told him that she'd never enter those rooms if someone was in there. "Thank you for that. If you need anything, bedding though I'm not sure how that would work, you tell one of us, and we'll get it for you."

"Thank you." She did tell him of a few things that she might need soon. Mostly, it was scraps of yarn and material they could use for blankets. Wood splinters they could carve for tools. A lot of things that he remembered his grandma saving all the time. "You are right in thinking that your granny saved a great deal for us. There is a can in your own kitchen that she used. I believe that your brother gave it to you for a remembrance. However, it has been closed now, and we are unable to get into it for the treasures there. If you could open it enough that we can slip in and out of it, we would be ever so grateful to you."

"I'll do that now." He closed the lid on the grill and watched as several hundred of the little creatures came closer to it. They were warming themselves up, he could see and invited them into his home. "Just be careful of the fireplace, and I'll light it for you."

After opening the can that they told him about in the kitchen, he dug out other things that he knew his granny had saved, to which he'd been saving as well. A habit that he'd only just come to realize he was still doing from his childhood.

Twist ties from things that they ordered online. Small rubber bands. Safety pens and pieces of crayons. All things now that he had met the little ones, he could see usefulness for. As he was headed to the living room to start a fire, it was Thad who was telling his mom that they were going to need to buy sugar cubes as well as dried fruit.

~*~

Rusty held her son to her breast as she fed him. All she could think about was how lucky she'd been in being found. The baby, her little Joey, had been breached and had the Cross family now shown up when they had, she was sure that she would have died and he along with her. Hugging him tightly to her again once he was finished feeding, she stood up and put him into his makeshift bed.

The Cross family had been so generous with their time and magic. Rusty knew about magical creatures and shifters. Her great uncle, now long gone, had been a hawk. His mate, she had heard, was just human and had died long before he had. Uncle Raymond had told her of his adventures as a shifter, the way to tell them apart from humans that they worked or mingled with. She knew a great deal more than she thought most humans did about sharing space with someone who wasn't at all like they were.

The knock at the door had her pulling her gown

up and over her naked breasts. She wasn't a prude, but she knew that there were children in the house. Great kids who had been helping her out since she arrived. As well as they saved her and Joey's life. After bidding the person to come in, she smiled at Belle.

"We're about to have dinner. Dad sent me up here to see if you'd join us. And Mom said that if you wanted a shower before dinner, I can watch Joey for you." She said that she'd just fed him so he'd sleep. "Okay then. You take a shower and stuff, and then we'll go down together."

"I'd love a shower." Almost too giddy with the idea of being cleaned up, she gathered up what she would need while talking to the little girl. "If he wakes up, just call for me. I can come right out if he's fussy. Otherwise, just let him lay there until he cries. Which he doesn't do much, but he might if—"

"Ms. Rusty, please go take a shower before he wakes up." They were both laughing when she went to the bathroom. Closing the door, she decided to leave it open just enough that she could hear Belle if she needed her. After brushing her teeth three times while the water got warm enough for her, she stepped under the powerful spray.

Just letting the water roll over her felt like heaven. She'd been getting washed up for the last few days instead of a full shower, and this was much needed. Her long hair needed a good scrubbing, too, and there was some lovely-smelling shampoo to do that. Rusty felt so good that she washed her hair three times before she decided it was as clean as it was going to get.

Losing track of time, she hurriedly dried and wrapped the towel around her body. Slipping into the bedroom to tell Belle how sorry she was, Rusty encountered a man sitting in the rocking chair, talking to her son. He looked up at her just as she was ready to scream the house down.

"My name is Barron Cross. My brother Gibb lives here with his wife, Maddy. They have three children, who I love too, by the names of Thad, Belle and Maria. I'm not going to hurt either of you. I came up here to see if Belle needed something, and she said that you were taking a shower." He spoke to her in a calm, soft voice; however, he looked at Joey. "He started to fuss a little bit, and I didn't want to make you end your shower if you weren't ready, so I've been telling him about the mountain that he was living on as well as some of the things that I've gotten done today."

"He's staring at you like he's listening to every word." Barron laughed and said that he'd been thinking the same thing. "I'm sorry that I took so long. It's just that it felt so good to be clean."

"I understand. Sometimes, when I'm working, it's all I can do to make it home and get cleaned up. It's really nice, too, just to shower so that you can wash all your worries off your shoulders. I'm thinking that you have a lot of that, too." She said she did but wasn't stressing about it so much coming here. "Good for you. I've spoken to Howard, Joey's biological father—just so you know, he doesn't have any idea where you are, but I wanted to talk to him about his wife's father. She is trouble."

"You've no idea." She heard her belly growling and knew that he'd heard it too. "I'm betting that I missed dinner. That's my own fault for taking a long shower. Belle did tell me that they were having burgers."

"They've waited on you. And to be honest, you weren't in there all that long." He finally looked at her. "Why don't you get dressed, and the three of us will head to the dining room. There is another bassinet in there for you to have Joey close in the event that he needs you again."

"I'll have to change him." Barron said he'd done that already and that he'd put him in a warm sleeper. "Thank you. You didn't have to do that. You guys have already opened your home for me. I don't want to think you have to take care of us too."

"It was my pleasure to help out. He's a cute little man, I think. And lucky for both of us, since I've never changed a baby before, there were instructions on the box on how to do it." She laughed with him, telling him how she'd had to refer to the box as well. "That made me feel better. Hurry up, and we'll head down."

She closed the door this time as she stripped off the towel. The clothing that she'd brought in with her was nice, nicer than she would have purchased for herself. As she was brushing her hair, she heard Joey fussing and nearly went out to take care of him when Barron laughed.

"He's just telling me that he's pooped this time. Little bugger. I've got him." The whistling startled her. What man would willingly change a poopie diaper on a child that he didn't know? But then, she knew that the Cross men were supposed to be the nicest men in the world. She only heard that about a million times since coming here.

Maddy was drying her legs when she felt a bump under her skin. Trying to see what it was nearly had her falling on her head, so she decided to get help from Barron. Knowing full well that he'd not find a woman who had only just given birth a week ago sexy, she made her way out to him with her shirt and panties on.

"Can you tell me what this is?" He just stared at her, so she gave him a little shove. "This thing here. They told me when I woke up after the implant that they'd accidentally cut me. It's always been there, I guess, but now I worry about what it could be."

"Yes, sure. I can do that." Rusty turned around when he asked her to. His warm fingers touching her flesh made her warm all over and also embarrassed her. When he asked her if she'd had surgery recently, she told him again what they'd done when she went in to have the insemination done. "It's a device."

"What sort of device?" He asked her if he could take it out. "Yes. Do you know what it—ouch. That fuck…that hurt. What did you do?"

"I cut it out." When she turned to yell at him about warning her next time, she looked at the pill-shaped thing that was in his hand. "Do you know what this is, Rusty?"

"No." She looked at his face. "But you do, don't you? I mean, you cut it out of me without figuring out what it is, so I'm guessing that it's bad and that you know just what it is. It's something bad, isn't it?"

"Not now, it's not." She nodded and waited. "It's a tracking device. You said that they put you under when they did the procedure, correct? My thinking is that someone, Paige, more than likely had them place this under your skin so that she could keep track of you. Not just where you are, but I'm betting that if we have someone look at this, they'll tell us that it's also something to track your health. Like your heart, the baby. Even if you're well or not."

Rusty sat down on the bed. Her thoughts were all jumbled up, but it was clear that Paige had had this done to her. But why? Up until last month, she'd been —

"Don't worry about it right now. I'm going to have it looked at, and then you can make a plan as to how you want to handle this. All right? Get dressed, and we'll go down and have a meal with my family. Then and only then will we worry. It's there. It's been there for at least nine months, so there is no point in getting worried about it after this time." She looked up at him when he stood over her. "Come on, Rusty. No one will hurt you or Joey. Get dressed, then we'll see what we can find out."

Nodding, she made her way back to the bathroom to finish getting dressed. Turning to look at Barron, she thought of the one thing that had been on her mind since he'd told her it was a tracking device.

"I don't know why, but I believe that there is an explosive in that, too. So that…so that I can die if I don't play well with her." He didn't say anything, and that worried her more. "She wanted me to terminate my pregnancy when I spoke to her last month. My due date had been less than a month away. Paige told me that I either get rid of the baby or she'd get rid of us both. She honestly meant that, I think now."

"Get dressed, honey. She can't hurt you now." Nodding again, she went into the bathroom, suddenly afraid to shut the door behind her. As she pulled on her pants and socks, she tried her very best not to think about Paige. The woman was off her rocker if she thought that she was going to kill her little boy. There wasn't any way that she'd cause harm to someone who was innocent in all of this.

Chapter 7

Maddy wasn't entirely sure that she liked having the little people around all the time. It wasn't that they weren't helpful to her and the kids while Joey was gone, but they were just too helpful, too. Like she had wanted to wash a load of towels to be able to hang them out on the line.

"Where are the towels that were in the washer?" They also vibrated loudly when asked something. It didn't matter what it was; just asking would get them excited. "I was going to hang them out on the line today. It's warmer than it has been, and I thought that it would feel good to use them."

"Oh, my lady. We've dried them with magic and put them away for you. It is our pleasure to do so for you and the others." Strawberry was the one that seemed to be in charge. Though, if you asked her if she was, she would say that it was a collective decision. Like that show from a long time ago that was collectively taking over people's minds. "I can get them wet again if you wish for us to hang them outside. Though, that would make them stiff, don't you think?"

"It's all right." Maddy knew that they'd do that too. Mess something up when she'd been about to do it. "Where are the kids? Are they still doing their homework?"

"Yes, my lady." That really wasn't what she wanted to hear, but she let it go. As she was making her way to the kitchen to have a cup of tea, she was told to have a seat, and the cup she'd been using, as well as the tea in it, were just there. Like a lot of things that she'd been wanting to do over the last few days. "Would you like some scones? They're fresh this morning."

"No, thank you. I think that I want to just sit here and relax." They didn't understand that either, she'd come to discover. Relaxing wasn't something that they did. If they weren't busy-busy-busy, they were figuring out ways to make themselves busy. "Do you think that I could just have a few minutes alone?"

"Yes, my lady." She didn't care for the my

lady bit either, but getting them to stop was next to impossible. Maddy turned to look at the little person she'd spoken to.

She could almost feel her hurt. And there was no doubt that she had hurt the little being. Sighing heavily, she turned in her seat and looked at her. Really looked. She was the most beautiful creature that she'd ever seen.

"I bet the flowers that you worked with were the best in the bunch. Does your red coloring mean that you only worked with the red ones?" She told her what the red color meant. "Oh. Well, that explains a great deal. It's a sign of your promotion in your realm. What's the highest you can attain?"

"Red, my lady. As red at the sunlight as it falls over the mountain into the next evening. The sky, when it's trying, just one more time to show off before it goes to the other side of the world. I think it's like that for us to remember that tomorrow will be just as bright and happy." Maddy told her that was beautiful. "The sun and the weather are our most treasured things. Without either, we'd no longer have magic in the world. Without the flowers, there would be no more people either. Things have a special order. And we're only here to help with that."

"Thank you for everything that you do." Strawberry bowed before her. "We have to work something out with the house, however. I love that you're all here and that you want to help out. But for me, it's too much. I'm not used to it."

"I wondered if that was going to be something that we'd work on. They're so happy to have someone to serve and help. We meant no harm." Maddy told her again that she was sorry and that she knew that they'd not meant anything by being super helpful. "If you would allow it, my lady, we can make sure that the house is in tip-top shape all the time. Beds made, laundry too. We do that for you so that you can have more time to spend with Lord Gibb and the children. We so love too that you're breeding. Another infant in the house will give you so much magic here. Children, especially babies, give us a boost of energy and magic that keeps us happy. You, too, if you would only allow us to give it to you."

"What do you mean, give it to me? I didn't know that there was magic that came to me as well. You know that I'm only human, correct?" Strawberry told her that she might well have been human when she came to be with Lord Gibb, but she wasn't any longer. "Because we bonded."

"Yes. And you love him. He loves you as well."
She smiled, and Strawberry smiled back at her. "It is
written on your face how much you love him. It's a
sight that we, as faeries, don't see often. Not the pure
love that the two of you have."

"I've never thought of it as being anything but
love. But I do know that I will never love anyone else
but him. He, really, he's the only man that I've ever
met that makes me want to be around him all the
time." Strawberry told her that she had such a love
at one time. "I'm sorry. You lost him."

"I did. Long ago now that I don't remember his
voice, but I do remember how he told me daily how
much that he loved me. That he would forever be
there for me. Then a monster in the form of a human
found him with the flowers we were all attending
to and killed him. He gave his life so that the rest
of us could escape as the monster meant to kill us
all." Maddy felt her heart melt for the girl. It hurt
her to think that the poor woman was alone but for
her family. Maddy told her again how sorry she was.
"You are a kindness that I've never encountered
before, my lady. Thank you for your kindness about
my Slate."

For the rest of the morning and into the late

afternoon, the two of them worked on a plan that would keep everyone happy. Now that she knew how much the little people depended on the household to keep them out of trouble, she was a little bit better about them being around all the time. They also set up an area in the house where the faeries could go to rest and call home.

"The bedroom is lovely, my lady. And all the windows will help us be warmed by the sun." The windows had only been about two feet by two feet when they picked out the room. But with the magic that she now shared with Strawberry, there were not only more of them, but they were as long as the wall and wider as well. "I like the idea of having the baskets around for things that you find for us. Some of the things that you suggested, we've never had before. I think that the smaller nails will serve us well for making tools."

The baskets had been created by her as well. And since they were labeled with what items could go into each of them, she thought that the children would be able to enjoy helping as well. Things like small stones, twist ties and other things like scraps of material were only a few things that they could give to them. The fact that they would bring things to her when they needed them glued together was something that she thought would be fun for her, too. And the watercolor and paints were a huge hit with the other faeries.

By the time they had exhausted all the ideas that they could, she sat down on the couch to catch a nap. She knew that she should be doing something, but Maddy was mentally drained. A feeling that she'd never experienced before today. But it had been fun working with the others. It was something that she thought she could do daily, even at the shop she was running.

Smiling, she thought of the A Cross to Bear shop. Even the name, even if you didn't know that the Cross family were bears, was something that she loved. But being able to go there daily and run the place like she was, it was a dream come true for her.

Strawberry had suggested that she send some faeries to the place to 'tidy up' at the end of the day. The place was huge, too. Three floors of nothing but things for tourists to purchase. And since Fraizer had finished up the table and had it put in a prime location, more people were coming in to see it.

It was Maria who had suggested putting a tall sign out front to alert people that they had new merchandise in. Restocks too of the peoples' favorites. Like the tea and the arrowheads that had been found around their land. Everyone contributed something to the place. Even her kids had been putting some of their artwork in to sell as well. Her cell phone ringing had her smiling when she noticed it was from the shop.

"Ms. Maddy, there is a couple here that want to purchase Mr. Frazier's table. They want us to arrange to have it shipped to them. I've already made sure that they know the price — like four times as well as made sure that they understand that they're paying for the transport." She heard a door close, and the sounds of the shop were cut off. "These people are crazy mad for that table, ma'am. They told me that they'd been here three times to look it over and decided that it would be perfect in their home in Montana. I tried to call Mr. Fraizer to come and sign it, but he's not answering. I'm as nervous as I've ever been with a sale. It's a huge sale, and they're gonna pay with cash so they can get it shipped to their home in time for Thanksgiving."

"Shipping will be a great deal. Did you tell them that it weighs about nine hundred pounds?" Carol said that she had a lot. "All right. I'll be there soon. I'll also try and get in touch with Fraizer. He's going to wet his pants over this. He said it would never sell. That's why the price is so high. All right. I'm on my way."

She was in her car when she reached out to Frazier. He sounded frustrated, and she told him how sorry she was to have interrupted him. He laughed a little and told her that it wasn't her fault that he was so far behind today. Maddy didn't ask why. She had a feeling he was late for the same reason that she was late getting out of the house every day. Sex.

"I'm all right. What can I do for you, my dear?" She told him about the sale of his table. "I'm sorry? You're joking, right? No one is going to pay that much for—you are joking, right?"

"I'm not. I'm headed there now to figure out the shipping of it. They want it in their home by the holiday." He laughed and told her that was a good one. "Fraizer. I promise you, I'm not joking. That is where I'm headed, and if you could go there too, they want to meet the artist."

"That table took me eight years to finish. I mean, once I got started on it again after a long delay, it didn't take me that long. After making all the little pieces of our mountain—Maddy, that table is marked at fifteen grand. They know that, don't they?" She told him what Carol had told her about telling them four times. "I didn't think it would sell. I mean, I guess that's the whole point in putting a price on it, but I never thought that—this is a joke, right? I'm on my way there, but I'm having trouble wrapping my head around it selling."

The table was worth every penny that he had it priced for. Fraizer had picked up things from the mountain to make it a one-of-a-kind table.

After carving wooden pieces, picking up tiny stones and moss, and drying small branches that he turned into trees, he built log cabins along the mountain, even going so far as to put his parents' as well as his recently lost grandparents' names on the headstones in the family cemetery. The rivers that ran down the mountain that supplied water to the homesteads were made of glass. Styled to perfection by Dexter, who even sharded up some of the blueish pieces and put them into the water to make the waterfalls. Salmon were depicted in the scene by hand-painted layers. To make the fish appear to be jumping from the waters as bears were set there to catch them had taken Fraizer hours of pouring and painstakingly painting each layer. The entire scene was then covered in resin to make it look as if you could step right into the scene and be a part of their everyday lives.

Fraizer was there before she was. When she got out of her car, she asked him why he'd not gone in. The look he gave her was one of disbelief. Like he was still thinking she was pulling a fast one on him by telling him a lie about the table being sold.

"All right. When we get in there, don't you dare ask them if they really want to buy it. I'll smack you around so hard that your children's children will still be reeling from it. Understand?" He said that he did. "Good. Now, you put on your professional face and talk to these people. I mean what I said, too. I will hurt you."

"You're mean." She thanked him. "I told the others that it was sold, and they're coming too. Someone is going to have to help load it on the truck. Which, in a fit of still disbelief, I have made arrangements to have it picked up."

"Thank you." As soon as they entered, the couple, a younger couple that looked like they were so in love, came to talk to Fraizer. As she made her way to the table to make sure that it was still in great shape, she saw that all the others had shown up as well. Mark was laughing when she told him that Fraizer still didn't believe her that it had sold. "He'll just have to make something else to replace it, I'm thinking."

"Yeah, that'll be easy to get him to do now that this one sold. However, it'll never be like this piece." She said that she had hoped not. Mark ran his hands over the smooth, glossy surface. "I knew that it would sell eventually. Not this soon — How long has it been in here? A month?"

"About that. I thought it would sell someday. Just needed to have the right person or, in this case, the right couple come along." As the trucking company showed up, measuring and getting an approximate weight, Mr. Lonne came to talk to them. The man was as excited as she was to have it in his home. "These men will be delivering the table for you. You will need to make sure that they know where to go. Also, you'll pay them directly."

"Yes, that's a good idea. Mrs. Cross, you've made our lives with this. We've been in here four times already to talk about it. Finally, I told my wife that we could keep visiting it or just have it in our home. I love the idea of having our families over for the holidays and this being in our dining room. There are some other pieces that I'm going to be having taken home as well."

While Mr. Lonne talked to the shipping company, she helped Carol with the sale. Since Fraizer was here, he approved a ten percent discount on it for paying in cash. Who the fuck carried around that much money on the off chance of buying a table. Not that she really cared, but really?

The other items that they purchased — a dining wear set with twenty place settings. Actually, it had been two for ten people, but it was great to see them going to a good home. There were kitchen items, the matching canister set to the tableware, and a teapot with enough tea cups to go around. There was a cheese board that Fraizer had made, too, that they simply had to have.

The table being moved out had drawn quite a crowd of people. They made more sales while the table was being wrapped up than they'd done the previous day. Also, Carol was able to get a new thing that was being offered off to a good start. It was having purchases — after being paid for, of course — delivered to where the people were staying for a fee.

"I think that the closer we get to Christmas, we should offer gift wrapping. If you can find some paper that looks like it's a scene from around here, I mean." She had an idea that one of the family could design some unique wrapping paper and have it printed. It would be worth it to see how people reacted to that. "Also, you might think this is weird. I thought we should put out a jar for money to go to the Alford and Minnie Cross Scholarship fund. They would have loved that."

"I love that idea." Mark told Carol that if she found a jar now, he'd put the first donation in it. As soon as the jar was set behind the counter to be labeled, Mark put in a hundred dollars. "Granny and Grandda, they would have loved this idea, like you said. But I think too that they'd be really embarrassed for someone making a big deal about them passing. Thank you, Carol, for thinking of this. Hopefully, we'll be able to send a few extra bucks to college with some lucky kids."

Maddy didn't know why, but she thought that the jar would be filled several times over the next few months. The Crosses had been well loved and adored by everyone that they met. It was a shame that they'd died recently. But she also knew from the family that they were happy together on the mountain in the sky, too.

~*~

The greenhouse was doing well with selling trees. It was mostly locals that he was selling to. A couple of them had told him that they'd been waiting for him to branch out with trees. Most of them just wanted to put some fruit trees in their yard. Gibb didn't voice his concerns over that. Bears loved apples.

He'd never imagined that anyone would want to buy trees this time of year, but as soon as they got a new shipment in, they'd be out the door. Going over the books, Ewing came to visit him. They made plans to get some dinner together as Maddy was having a girls' night out with the other wives.

"Did I tell you that I've been spending time with Rusty and Joey?" He turned to look at his brother. "Nah, she's not my mate. Barron's, either, if you were going to ask. We just wanted her to feel welcome, and she's really a nice woman. And the little guy is fun to be around. Have you got to see him stretch? Christ, Gibb. It's got to be the most beautiful thing you'll ever witness. Anyway, she's a smart cookie herself. I was talking to Mark about hiring her to go over the books for us. Rusty has a master's in accounting. Her passion is numbers."

"I thought, well, I guess I had hoped that she'd

be a part of the family." Ewing said she might well be yet. "What do you mean? You're not serious about her, are you? That would be wonderful."

"No. Not us but David. I don't know if he realizes it yet, but he's about as in love with her as you are one of your kids." He asked him what he meant. "I think he thinks of Rusty as the child he never had. And he goes ape over little Joey. Yeah, I can see the two of them hooking up like father and daughter. They're making plans to move in together, as father-daughter, as soon as this business with Paige is over with. Have you heard anything more about that device you found?"

"It's a tracker. And Rusty was right. It did have components in it to make it explode. As close as it was to her artery, I think she would have bled out had it gone off. I'm sure that was the plan." Ewing said that was just sick. "I know. Also, I've heard from Howard. He's a nice enough guy. I mean, he's pretty beaten up about how this is all going on, but he's going to go to court with Rusty to turn full custody of Joey over to her. And he's paying her the money that she was promised too. That's pretty stand-up if you ask me."

"It is. When are they going to hook up?" He

told him that they'd arrested Paige just yesterday. "Really? Great. On what charges? I'm assuming that you can't prove that she tried to kill Rusty about the child, can you?"

"I don't know what's going on with that. Mark hired an attorney for her, and she's working closely with Mark. I don't remember her name, but Mark said that she comes highly recommended in cases like this." Ewing asked a couple more questions that he didn't have an answer for when he opened up his computer to order more trees. "I do know that the device has been looked over by the top people in DC. Sunny is having some experts come in and talk about the thing tomorrow. I'd like to know that this woman isn't going to hurt anyone else."

"Yeah, me too. To think that she wanted to kill her own child. The little guy isn't at a point where he could piss anyone off, and there she was wanting Rusty to abort that. I think for as far along as she was, isn't that considered murder?" Gibb told him that he wasn't sure. "You don't know a hell of a lot for having the woman staying in your home, dumbass. What good are you anyway?" Gibb laughed.

"I'm a man that stays out of the affairs of women. As you pointed out, Rusty is a smart woman;

she and Joey are safe here, and that was my main goal in having her stay. I will and have helped her when she asked. But for the most part, I stay out of it." Ewing said he was a coward. "You bet your life I am. Especially with the women in this family. Have you noticed that they do things together? All we need to do is piss one of them off, and we'll have all of them angry with us. I'm staying out of it until asked. And when I am asked, I do what they want. I'm also a smart man in knowing that I'm stupid compared to all of them. Also, I think that they could kick my ass without any trouble should I step out of line. No. I have two daughters, a female houseguest as well as a wife. I'm learning my place and sticking to it."

"Pussy." They both laughed. "However, I do see your point. I said something the other day to Jamie, and before I could get home, all four of them were up my butt about it. I only meant it as a joke, but it didn't go over well. I guess you might be right."

"I am right. And when your mate comes, and I believe we're all going to have mates before the end of the year, I suggest you get into the habit of saying, *what can I do to help you* instead of saying, *here, let me do that for you*. I swear, you'll thank me for it." As they made their way to the little deli restaurant that had just opened up, they talked about the holidays. "I'm putting up a huge tree. Thad and I have already been scouting around the woods for the biggest one we can find. I never thought of having kids at Christmas time. It's a good deal more fun for me since I was just a kid."

The two of them were still talking about both holidays coming up and what they were going to do to their home after ordering dinner. Ewing was the one who usually decorated his home, and the others would just admire his. But this year and from now on, Gibb was going to be outdoing his brother at every step. He and the kids had been looking at all the blowup things every chance they got. It was going to be epic, he knew.

After dinner, he and his brother went to his home. The faeries weren't around where Ewing could see them, and he was sort of disappointed that he couldn't share the news about them with his family. He'd have to find someone to talk to about it. All this good fortune, and it was for his family, could be helping them out as well. But it hadn't been his decision to make, and he was going to follow the rules.

Maddy coming home with the kids made him

happy. Thad helped him clean up the living room. They'd made a slight mess having a popcorn tossing contest and were telling him about staying at Mark's house. He'd allowed the kids to pick up all the scrap wood that had been left over from the construction crew, and Thad was excited to learn how to carve wood.

"You already have the basis down." Ewing did a little carving as well, and he was giving Thad some of his old tools tomorrow. "When you play around with the rocks and shining them up, you'll be able to do the same with the wood. Making pieces that will last a lifetime for you."

When the two of them wandered off to his workshop, he went to the kitchen to find Maddy. That was usually where she ended up at the end of the day. Kissing her on the back of the neck while she talked to the girls, he sat down and took a couple of carrots off of Belle's plate while he listened. Maddy asked him what he thought.

"I wasn't paying attention." She tsked at him. "I'm sorry. I was thinking about different things today—to which I got a great deal done, thank you very much, and I didn't tune in to hear what you said. But I want you to know that I agree with your side one hundred percent."

Belle laughed and said she was going to her room. Maria just rolled her eyes at him as she, too, left him. Confused about what was going on, he asked Maddy. She sat down and looked so sad that he wanted to slay dragons for her. Instead, he held her hands while she explained.

"Maria wants to go to an all-girls school that she read about online. I've looked into it. It's a good school, and they offer more things than just your standard classes. There is horseback riding as well as lots of different art classes. But it's so far away." He asked her where it was. "England. I want her to go, I do, but then I don't, too. She'll not be right here where I can hug her when I want. I know that we can talk every day and even video chat, but what if something happens? I won't be there."

"Why not?" She asked him what he meant. "I mean, with Amelia around, just popping over to see her would be easy enough. In fact, you and Maria should pop over there and have a good look around the school together. I know you looked it up, that's great, but that's not like being there in person. I'm not trying to get rid of either of you. But she might find that it's not what she thought it was when she's actually there."

"What if it's everything that she thought it was? She'll want to go." Gibb, ever the diplomate, asked his mate what was really bothering her about this. "She doesn't seem to mind that she'll be thousands of miles away." When she started to cry, he was happy that he'd not laughed at her concern.

"Look. She's only ten right now. By the time she's old enough to leave home, you're going to be twice as bad about her leaving. And I'm betting that she's more concerned about leaving her family behind than you think she is. Maria is the tender one. She'll be calling you every day, and by the time she's there for a few months, you'll both be wondering what all the fuss was about."

"I'll miss her." He told her that he would as well. "I know you will. That's what I love about you. You're their father, through and through. And I love you for it."

"You couldn't have said anything in the world that makes me feel this good." When the front doorbell rang, he was on his way to get it when several hundred faeries beat him to it. Strawberry told him to not open the door wider than he had to. "Who is it, do you know?"

"Paige Crawford." That was enough that he backed away from the door a bit. "You will be safe, my lord. Just don't allow her to come in. We will kill her if she does."

"Yes, all right." He opened the door then when it sounded like she was lying on the buzzer. "What do you want? And how did you get out of jail?"

"Oh, nice to meet you too. Where is my baby oven? I want you to bring her to me right now, or so help me, I'll have you arrested for harboring a fugitive." He asked her what she was talking about. "Rusty. She's got my child, and I want her to turn it over as soon as it's born. Where is she? I know she's here."

"Because you put a tracker on her?" Paige just smiled. "Yes, well, that's been removed from her, I've heard. Also, you'll be thrilled to know that the Feds are looking it over now. You never answered me. How did you get out of jail?"

"I paid the pricey fee to be free. Since you seem to know about the tracker, you must know where she is. I demand that you bring her here so that I can talk to her." He heard someone behind him and knew that it was Rusty when he smelled her. "There you are. Oh, and look at you. Where is my baby? I want him."

"Two months ago, you told me that you didn't. Now, all of a sudden, you want him. Make up your mind. Besides, he's not anything to you. You were never a doner for him." She said that her husband was his biological father. "Yes, he is. So, since you two are divorced, then it's more his child than yours. And I'm not going to give him up for any amount of money."

"Everyone says that, but if the price is high enough, you'll take it. And you'll be happy to get it. Where is the brat? I want you to bring him here, and I'll pretend like you didn't take off with my goods." Rusty laughed. Gibb reached out to his family to let them know what was going on. All of them said they were on their way. "All you had to do was abort him when I told you to. But no, you got squeamish about it. There is no way that he would have felt a thing if you'd just allowed me to knock you down the stairs, and he'd be gone. Christ, you're causing me all kinds of trouble here. Hand him over, now, Rusty, or I'm calling the police."

"I've already done that." Paige asked Rusty what she was talking about. "Calling the police. I've called them. You don't have to worry about doing it yourself since I know that you hate to lift your finger to do any of the dirty work that seems to follow you around all the time. I've been busy while keeping my baby safe. It's amazing what you can find out with a good internet connection."

"What the hell are you talking about? Just hand the baby over." Rusty pulled a sheet of paper out of her backside pocket. "I guess you think that whatever you have there is going to make a difference to me."

"I should hope it does. I have a list of nineteen outstanding warrants for your arrest. Also, a great many departments across the United States where police are looking for you to answer a few questions about missing children. And a few adults. That's what the police are coming for. To arrest you on this new information that I've found." Paige started to back away from the door. Rusty laughed. "I'd not try to run if I were you. Those bears behind you look like they're hungry. I don't know if they like to play with their food before eating it, but I'm sure that if I asked, they'd do that for me. What do you think, Gibb?"

"I think you might be right. I think for the chance to hold onto your son, they might well do anything you asked of them." Rusty grinned like it was the best thing ever to find out that she could command five large black bears. "Ah, look. The police are here. And just in time, too. It looks like the bears are coming closer to see what all the bruhaha is about."

As Paige was taken away, Rusty sat in the living room talking to her son. David showed up a little while later and was glad, too, that Paige wasn't going to be any trouble. The way she was verbally abusing the cops on the way to the car made him think she wasn't going to have a good time this time in jail. They'd treat her as she was treating them. Time would tell how long she'd be in jail or prison for.

Chapter 8

Barron didn't want to be at this meeting. In fact, he thought that he could go his entire life, even being immortal, without having to be in the same room as the people that he was with. He'd told them countless times that he wasn't selling his business. And twice as many times as he'd told them, they countered with more of something.

More money. More perks. More of anything that they thought that he'd like. Which he kept telling them was to be left alone. They didn't seem to get that either. Why would he, according to them, be happy with the small amount of money that he was currently making when he could be making so much more. He looked at the man that had been doing the most talking.

"I'm happy. I don't want to get in over my head." He, Mr. Denver Longshot, told him that he'd never be in over his head because they would be there with all the help that he needed. "I don't need any help with my business right now. That's the way that I like it."

"Mr. Cross? Barron, can I call you that?" He told him that Mr. Cross was fine. "That's not too terribly friendly. I was hoping that we could get this settled up and you'd think of us as your family. A good family that is going to be making a great deal of money."

"I don't need any more family than the one I have right now. And I don't need to be making a great deal of money. I'm happy and content with the way things are going right now." He stood up, and so did Mr. Longshot. "Don't contact me again. If you do, I'm going to call my attorney and have you charged with harassment."

"Mr. Cross, you don't know what you're missing. We could be making you a millionaire in less time than it takes you to make a batch of this cheese." Barron turned to look at the man. His anger and his bear were getting the best of him. "You should just sit back down and let us start again. You're not hearing what we can offer you by letting us take care of things for you."

"I'm already a millionaire. I also don't need someone to take care of things for me. I'm a grown man, not some sniffling kid who needs someone like you chasing me down like you are. Back the fuck off, or I call in the troops. And trust me when I tell you, you do not want me to have to call in the troops." He turned to the door again, and the man grabbed him and jerked him around. "Take your hands off of me."

"Look. Maybe we got off on the wrong foot, Barron. Let's start over as friends." When he jerked his arm free, the man grabbed him again. "You're not going to leave here until we come to some kind of understanding. And by that, I mean that you're going to let us help you make the kind of sales that you should be making. Think of the profit you'll be making if you would just get your head out of your ass and listen to what we're telling you."

"Frazier, I need you to come to me right fucking now." He didn't bother with their link but called for him to come to him now. When Fraizer showed up, he had Mark and Gibb with him. "This man has tried to detain me twice now by physically holding me from leaving. I would like to have charges pressed against him."

"All right, little brother." Mark looked at

Longshot. "Remove your hand from my brother, or I will. I'm not fucking with you right now. You do what I tell you, or else."

"Look, I was just telling your brother here that we got off on the wrong footing. He just needs to stay here and listen to us." Barron noticed that the other people in the room with them had backed off. They were so pressed against the furthest wall that they looked to be a part of it. Longshot turned and looked. "What are you idiots doing? We need his business. One of you come here and explain to him how much money he's going to be making."

"I think you should just let him go home. He obviously doesn't want to do business with you. And I'm not going to jail for you." Longshot asked the other man what he was talking about. "Did you do any research on this man before coming here? Or demanded that he come to this meeting? I did. I'd not fuck with him any more than you have already. Just let him go. He said no, and I believe that he means it."

"Douglas, get your ass over here and talk to him. I'm out of options." The woman said that she liked her ass just where it was, and she wasn't going to jail either. "Do you people understand that we're going to be fired if we don't bring in more business. Isn't that what we were told when we came here?"

"You said that he'd be an easy buyout because he's nothing but a country bumkin. I did try and point out that he'd graduated at the top of his class from Harvard. Several times. And if you would have read over the file that I gave you, you'd also have known that his family is well connected and not to be fucked with." The man, Barron, couldn't remember his name right now, looked at him. "I'm sorry, Mr. Cross. None of us thought that his tactics were going to work out. However, he forced us to come with him. You'll understand if we don't think that we want to be associated with him any longer. I hope."

"Leave." They did. Nearly knocking their leader down in the process. Taking Longshot's hand from his shoulder to remove it, Barron let a bit of his bear go so that he'd break a few of his fingers before he was finished. "I told you not to touch me."

Not only did the police show up, but there were a few Feds with them. Barron had explained to the people in the room that he was a Federal Officer and that they implying that he'd be arrested if he hadn't shown up was their first mistake. The final straw was manhandling him.

Longshot was arrested. Once he was in cuffs, Barron took that opportunity to call his boss. He finally had to go into another room so that he could hear over the man cursing him. Christ, all he'd wanted to do was make some fancy cheese and sausage from his goats and pigs to make a few extra bucks in the winter months.

"Caitlynne Royce speaking." Barron didn't wait for her to tell him anything more but started in on telling her what he'd had to endure today. Not only that, but to let her know that the Feds had arrested her man Longshot for abuse to a Federal Officer. He was on a roll, telling her all the things that he'd said to the man when she whistled. Barron had to jerk the phone from his ear. It had been that loud. "May I speak now? I'm so sorry you were treated that way, sir. Longshot was fired from this company several days ago. I haven't any idea why he set up a meeting with you when I told him to his face that he was no longer to mention that he ever worked here, much less going to meetings with people who have told him no. The very fact that he manhandled you doesn't surprise me, either. The man worked for my father before I took over, and my dad let him get away with too much. I don't roll that way. If you'd not mind, Mr. Cross, is it? I'd like to speak to the arresting officers. I have a few more things to add to his incarceration."

Laughing, he handed the phone to the officer who had had Longshot taken to the jail. He told his brothers what she'd said to him, and for some reason, every bit of his anger was gone. Barron didn't even feel like he'd wasted any of his time today after hearing Ms. Royce talking to the officers there with him.

"Jamie is pissed off that you called for Fraizer instead of her. Just to give you a heads up. Also, you should know that none of them are happy that they didn't get to rescue you from the clutches of the bastard." Barron said that he was fine, but then the man had jerked him around. "I think that would have pissed me off as well. I didn't even think you were going to go to this meeting. I thought you had already decided that you weren't going to sell."

"He told me that if I didn't come, he'd have me arrested. I was just curious enough about how he thought to pull that off that I came. It wasn't worth it. The man is certifiable. He actually told me that I'd be a millionaire before the end of the year." Mark told him that he was already one, several times over.

"Yeah, I don't think that he believed me."

He made his way home after that. Barron had been going to work in the cheese factory today, but his plans were flexible. Once he had fixed himself something to eat and went out onto his deck, he was feeling much better. The ringing of his cell phone didn't bother him as much as it might have had he not gotten things squared away with Longshot.

"Mr. Cross? This is Caitlynn Royce again. I'm sorry to disturb you so late, but I do have a few questions to ask you. I'm not going to try and sell you on anything, but just some curiosity. What is it you sell that had him so rabid about contacting you in the first place?" He told her about the products that he sold. "Are you, by chance, related to the Cross that makes wine?"

"He's my brother, Ewing. My other brother, Dexter, he blows glass and makes the specialty wines that Ewing makes." She said that they were all talented then. "I guess you could say that. We were, up until a few weeks ago, working for the National Park, the Smoky Mountains. But when our grandparents died, Grandda being killed by one of the guests here, we decided that it didn't hold the same appeal that it did for us before. I believe we're enjoying life again. Especially me."

"I can understand that. My father, he ran this company with a lax hand and an even less hand at keeping it running. There were so many people that I'd had to let go that I was afraid that I'd never get it up and running again. Then, just like that, snap. It just all started to fall into place. Longshot was the last hanger-oner." He told her that he had heard of her company, too. "I'm glad to hear that. Thank you for that. To be honest with you, Mr. Cross, I might be a tad responsible for having Longshot pursue you so hard. I was given a basket of Mountain items. They called them in a large raffle recently. I have been thoroughly enjoying everything that was in it, but especially the wine and crackers. I've never been much of a cheese person, but it's delicious, too. Especially on Granny's—your grandmother. She made the crackers, didn't she?" Barron laughed.

"Yes. As you said, we're a talented family. Granny did make the crackers that we sell. Granny's Crackers are nearly sold out as soon as they hit the shelf here. I'll send you some when you run out. And I'll send some wine too if there is any left with this recent batch." She laughed and said that she'd be delighted to have them. "I'll see about getting it to you soon. Is there anything else I can do for you? It would be my pleasure since you didn't get Longshot out of his predicament."

"Longshot can rot in hell for all I care about him. He actually told me that he wouldn't normally listen to a woman boss, but he did out of respect for my father. My father. He was a good dad but had no head for business. I'm going to miss him." Barron told her that he was sorry for her loss. "I am as well. We were all we had for the longest time and—I'm sure you don't want to hear about this. Anyway. I have to travel down your way in a few days. I have to talk to the Feds about what Longshot did in the name of my company. The little shit even wanted me to pay to have him bailed out. Nope, not going to happen. But I do need to go there and prove that he wasn't working for me at the time. Do you know of any good places to stay while there?"

The two of them spoke for the next four hours. It was fun for him to have someone who didn't know the dynamics of his family to talk to her about it. He cried when he told her how his grandda had been killed and that his granny, so in love with him, died the same night. Barron told her about his goats, all seventy of them and how he had named them all as soon as they came to him.

Caitlynn told him about her father's lack of business sense as well as the things that they did when he wasn't working. It was the most enjoyable hours he'd spent on a date in a long time, and he told her that.

"For me as well. People hear that I'm a business owner, and they immediately think that I can get them a job. Not by working, mind you, but an income for them. Then they figure that I'm easy. Because, of course, that's the only way that a woman can get to the top of the ladder is by sex." She laughed. "I've been carrying a gun since I was old enough to carry one, and it's all that stands between me and some bad dates going seriously wrong."

It was nearly midnight when he made his way to his bed. He was exhausted, but it was more than that when he went to bed that night. Barron had been so stressed lately about nearly everything, but tonight, he felt like he could take anything on and be all right. Closing his eyes, he thought of the things that he was going to have to do tomorrow and didn't feel the normal dread that he did. It was nice, he thought, to have a shoulder to lean on. And Caitlynn had been good at it.

~*~

Gibb waited for the people to disembark from the plane before he held up his sign. Barron had had an emergency, or he would have been here to pick up the woman that he'd been talking about nonstop for two days now. When she smiled at him—or he hoped that was her—Gibb reached for her bag and told her who he was and why he was there.

"The gardener with three children and one on the way." He told her that was right. "Your brother told me a great deal about his family. I feel like we're all old friends by the way he talked about you. I was dreading this trip, I was, but I'm actually excited to be here. I hope his emergency isn't that bad. Is it one of his animals? He loves them a great deal."

"It is as a matter of fact. Bessy, I think that was the one who was breeding, and she went into labor earlier this morning. But she wasn't doing well, and he had to call the vet in. You're right about saying that he loves his animals. He takes good care of them, too." She said that he more than likely took better care of them than some people do their families. "I'm sure you're right about that. We've seen our fair share of mistreatment in our previous line of work."

"I'm sorry that you don't see a better side of

all of us. Barron told me that you're all shifter bears. I have some shifters working for me at the shop." They were headed to the car when he heard from his brother.

"I'm not going to be fit to talk to her today. Bessie and her baby died. There was no saving them, the vet said." He could hear the pain in his brother's voice, and it hurt him so badly. "Tell her that I'll see her later. I have to take care of the mamma and baby here before I can leave."

Gibb told Caitlynn what was going on. She asked if she could go to him, to be with him, and Gibb didn't ask his brother if that would be all right. Taking her to the mountain and then up behind the barns, he saw Barron sitting on the outside of the pen, looking as forlorn as he'd ever seen any of them.

Before he could stop the car and explain to Caitlynn that he thought this was a mistake, his brother really was hurting, she got out of the car and made her way to him. About halfway up the mountain that the barn sat on, she pulled off her heels and tossed them behind her. Gibb sat in the car and watched the two of them.

She didn't seem to say anything when she walked up to his brother. Once she was standing in front of him, Barron surprised him. He pulled her closer to him and sobbed into her belly. Gibb felt his own heart hurt. The pain of his sobs cut him to the core of his body. When Caitlynn went down on her knees, still holding onto his little brother, Gibb knew that the two of them would be all right.

As he drove home, he decided to take Caitlynn's things to Barron's home. If she wasn't going to be staying there, it would be a simple thing for them to sort things out. Wiping at a tear that would occasionally fall, he thought about the things that Barron had told him about the young woman. Just as he was getting into his car again, he realized that she might be the one.

All his life, Barron had told them that he wasn't going to have a mate. It took them all teasing him to find out that it wasn't a mate that he didn't want but the idea of it. He wanted a life partner. Someone that he could spend his days with every day and still be able to have a conversation with, too.

He wanted a friend, a lover and someone that he could depend on. He, too, had wanted the same things for his partner. It just then occurred to Gibb that it was just what he had with his own mate. Maddy was all those things and more to him. Looking back at his brother's home, he realized something else.

Of all the brothers, Barron was the most prepared for a mate. His house had been finished for years. Updated just last year with new kitchen appliances as well as the carpets taken out. The wood floors throughout the house were beautifully done and polished. There was plenty of wood stacked along the fence line to keep the place warm for years if need be.

Gibb also knew for a fact that his brother's furniture was comfy, well made and something that blended in with the surrounding mountains as much as the man did. Of all of them, too, Barron was the most rugged man. The one that would go into the mountains to find what he needed and make it over all of them.

In that moment, he was jealous of his brother and his new…his partner. They could, and more than likely would be able to stay on the mountain forever and never leave for anything that would be purchased in town. If it wasn't from the mountain or made by them, then it wasn't necessary for the two of them to have. Getting in his car, Gibb was happy.

Reaching out to his own partner, he told Maddy what he thought was going on. How he thought that

Barron had met his match. Spending only a little bit of time with Caitlynne from the airport to here, he knew so much about her that he felt, as she said, that he'd known her forever. She was going to be the steading hand in the Cross family. She was going to be what Granny had been for them. The glue of the family. The one that would get them together again for holidays, even birthdays.

It was nearly supper time when he heard from Barron. He was all right. He and Cailynn had buried the little family and were going to chill at his home for a few days. Yes, he told him when he asked, Caitlynn was his partner. The one he'd been waiting on his entire life.

Sitting in his own living room that night, Gibb was excited for brother Ewing. The youngest of all of them and the last to find his mate. Things, just as his grandparents would tell them all the time, were moving on. There would be babies born on their mountain. Partners brought up there as well. The Crosses, generations of them, would never leave the mountain, and there would be land there for them forever. Gibb was a happy man.

Before You Go...

HELP AN AUTHOR

write a review

THANK YOU!

Share your voice and help guide other readers to these wonderful books. Even if it's only a line or two, your reviews help readers discover the author's books so they can continue creating stories that you'll love. Log in to your favorite retailer and leave a review. Thank you.

AWARD WINNING, BESTSELLING AUTHOR

Kathi Barton, a winner of the Pinnacle Book Achievement Award and a best-selling author on Amazon and All Romance books, lives in Nashport, Ohio, with her husband, Paul. When not creating new worlds and romance, Kathi and her husband enjoy camping and going to auctions. She can also be seen at county fairs with her husband, an artist and potter.

Her muse, a cross between Jimmy Stewart and Hugh Jackman, brings her stories to life for her readers in a way that has them coming back time and again for more. Her favorite genre is paranormal romance, with a great deal of spice. You can visit Kathi online and drop her an email if you'd like. She loves hearing from her fans. aaronskiss@gmail.com.

Follow Kathi on her blog: http://
kathisbartonauthor.blogspot.com/

www.ingramcontent.com/pod-product-compliance
Lightning Source LLC
Chambersburg PA
CBHW050324200626
46810CB00023B/2986